Dreamfire

Dreamfire

Nicole Luiken

Nicole Luiken

GREAT PLAINS
TEEN FICTION

Great Plains Teen Fiction
(an imprint of Great Plains Publications)
420 – 70 Arthur Street
Winnipeg, MB R3B 1G7
www.greatplains.mb.ca

Great Plains Publications gratefully acknowledges the financial support provided for its publishing program by the Government of Canada through the Book Publishing Industry Development Program (BPIDP); the Canada Council for the Arts; as well as the Manitoba Department of Culture, Heritage and Tourism; and the Manitoba Arts Council.

Design & Typography by Relish Design Studios Ltd.

Printed in Canada by Friesens

Library and Archives Canada Cataloguing in Publication

Luiken, Nicole
Dreamfire / Nicole Luiken.

ISBN 978-1-894283-88-5

I. Title.
PS8573.U534D74 2009 jC813'.54 C2008-906924-2

Mixed Sources
Cert no. SW-COC-001271
© 1996 FSC
FSC

ENVIRONMENTAL BENEFITS STATEMENT

Great Plains Publications saved the following resources by printing the pages of this book on chlorine free paper made with 100% post-consumer waste.

TREES	WATER	ENERGY	SOLID WASTE	GREENHOUSE GASES
10 FULLY GROWN	3,640 GALLONS	7 MILLION BTUs	467 POUNDS	877 POUNDS

Calculations based on research by Environmental Defense and the Paper Task Force. Manufactured at Friesens Corporation

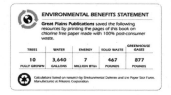

For my cousin, Karen, with thanks for her enthusiasm for this story.
It's mere coincidence that she is also the eldest of three sisters.

chapter one

The nightmare ambushed me in full daylight in the middle of Science class, of all places.

One moment I was hunched over the surprise quiz Mr. Darning had sprung on the class—my stomach in knots because I couldn't answer a single question—and in the next moment reality took a sudden sharp left turn.

Under my hands the test paper rippled. Black ink became variegated, shading from gray-black to raven. From flat to three-dimensional. I pulled back in alarm as the small spider diagram at the bottom of the page gathered its eight legs up from under it and crawled across my desk.

The spider was as big as my hand and gross looking. Repulsed, I watched as it used a line of silk to drop down onto the floor, and then scuttled towards the nearest corner.

Because my dad was a forest technologist, "Step on a spider, and it will rain," was something of a catchphrase with my sisters and me, especially during dry years like this one. It instantly became imperative to kill the spider.

I stretched out a foot and stamped down, but missed.

The spider curled itself into a protective ball, and I recognized the red hourglass shapes on the underside of its abdomen from a report I'd once done. Oh, crap, it was a black widow. I drew back, fearful of its poisonous bite. But I still wanted—needed—to kill it.

I had to make it rain.

Then I forgot all that because the spider molted. Its exoskeleton split in half and fell away. A new spider emerged from the old. Holy hell. It had tripled in size. It now came up to my knees, and was heading my way!

None of the other students seemed to see it. They remained bent over their tests, oblivious. Vulnerable.

I grabbed my stool and hurled it at the spider. I bowled it over, but did the freaky thing die? No. Instead another fracture line appeared on its body, and it molted again. This time when it got up, it was as big as a horse.

For a second fear paralyzed me, and the black widow took eight steps forward. "That's a good girl, Brianne," it croaked. "This won't hurt a bit." Silk spewed from the spinnerets on its huge abdomen, and it used the comb-like end of one hind leg to sling a loop of web at me.

Uh-uh. No way was that thing going to touch me.

I ducked under the table to avoid the sticky silk and came up in the row on the other side. I sprinted between the black tables, dodging still oblivious students and stools, while the spider clattered along behind me. I glanced back to see how close it was—too close—and veered towards the door. I didn't see its web until it was too late; I hit it full tilt.

The gauzy-looking strands gave under the impact, then snapped backward like a rubber band. Desperately, I tried to free myself, but drops of glue on the silk stuck to my arms and legs, holding me fast. The more I twisted, the more entangled I became. I began to pant. Not good.

The spider approached and examined me with eight cold, black eyes. Its stare hypnotized me. "It's not going to rain, Brianne. Your only chance to make it rain is to kill me. That's why I'm going to kill you!"

It reached for me with its front appendages. I screwed my eyes shut and turned my head aside, waiting for the black widow's fang to pierce my flesh and inject me with venom.

Something touched the back of my neck, and I screamed. I pushed violently away, but the web was no longer there, and I fell over backwards, still shrieking. I hit my head on the edge of a hard surface just before landing on my tailbone. Something thunked beside me, and I screamed a third time, certain it was the spider—except, why wasn't I already dead?

I cautiously opened one eye and saw a ring of avid faces peering down at me. No black widow spider, no web. I was still in Science 20 class, sprawled on the lab-room floor. I seemed to have fallen off my stool.

My face flamed in mortification, but I fought the tell-tale reaction, hiding my emotions as I'd learned to just over a year ago at my last school. If my nightmares were returning again, making a fool of myself in front of the entire class was the least of my worries. Grimly, I began to pull myself to my feet.

Someone grabbed my hand and helped me up. "Thanks," I said. A sense of inevitability rolled over me when I saw that the hand belonged to Benjamin Harper. It would have to be him; the absolute last person I wanted to see me like this. *Kill me now.* I braced myself, waiting for the curiosity, the what's-wrong-with-*her* look.

But Ben's face showed only concern. "Are you okay?"

I could have drowned in his blue eyes, and I was a shade slow in letting go of his hand. For a second I felt light-headed and not because of the blow I'd taken on the back of my head. *Benjamin Harper was worried about me.* Ben with his great smiles, friendly "Hi's," wavy brown hair, and tall, muscled body.

"I'm fine," I said automatically, then realized it was a lie. My head hurt, and my body was sore from the fall.

My speech, short as it was, opened the floodgates for the rest of the class to have their say.

"What happened? Why was she screaming?"

"Beats me. One minute Mr. Darning's talking, and the next she's screaming."

"Maybe she saw a mouse," one of the popular boys, Rex Tremont, suggested and laughter followed.

I gripped the solid edge of the lab counter with one hand and felt the back of my head with the other. No blood, but I felt nauseated, and the memory of the spider's hairy leg touching me made me shudder.

Then I saw the open textbook on my table. I glanced around. All the tables had open books and binders. No tests, face-down or face-up. The surprise quiz must have been part of the dream too, not just the spider. Talk about your small blessings.

"Hey, back off a little," Ben said, frowning at Rex. "Can't you guys see she's a little upset?"

That was such an understatement everyone laughed again. Mr. Darning shut them up. He was the principal as well as the science teacher, and his voice held unmistakable authority. "Everyone back to your seats. Do questions one to thirteen on page 103." Then to me, in a lower tone, "Can you walk, Brianne?" I nodded, but he didn't wait for an answer saying, "Ben, you help her to the nurses' office." My throat dried up.

A teacher was hurrying towards the three of us, and I could see a few curious heads peeking around doors up and down the hallway. "Everything's under control," Mr. Darning brusquely assured them and continued walking.

I tried to prepare myself on the way. What should I say? That I fell asleep and had a nightmare? That would seal my fate for sure in Mr. Darning's class. I slowed, and Ben took my arm in a firmer grip, helping me down the hall.

The school nurse checked my pupils for signs of concussion then took a look at my head. She parted my short brown hair away from the swelling with her fingers and tsked, "You've got a nasty bump, but the skin's not broken."

My head had started to throb, but I kept that off my face, too. I looked at Ben instead. He hadn't left the room as he might have, and I watched him until he caught me at it. Blushing, I looked around the sickroom. There wasn't much to it, just a cot and some cabinets.

I flinched. Up in the farthest corner hung a spider web, its threads glistening in the sunlight.

The nurse apologized, thinking she'd touched a tender spot, but I barely heard her. A scream tried to fight its way out of my throat.

C'mon, Brianne. Calm down, it was just a dream. And that's just a spider. A normal everyday spider like you see all the time. My nails dug into my palms as the spider moved. Just a dream. Sure. Just like all the rest were. Right?

Wrong. My dreams had a nasty habit of coming true.

Not that I was really expecting to be chased by a giant spider in real life. But the test? Oh yeah, that was coming, and the spider part would come true too, in some twisted way or another. Of that I had no doubt.

All too soon the nurse pronounced me fit, and Mr. Darning was looking at me across the desk in his office. "So Brianne," he said, "what was that all about?"

"I, um, was startled and lost my balance. I'm sorry about all the fuss." I offered him a weak smile. I wasn't a very good liar, but the truth was out of the question. Last year's fiasco had taught me that if nothing else.

Mr. Darning looked openly skeptical. "What *exactly* startled you? Why did you scream?"

"I saw a spider." My voice came out sounding hoarse.

Mr. Darning's eyebrows rose. "And are you in the habit of screaming at arachnids?"

I coloured. "No."

"It was a big spider," Ben put in unexpectedly. "I saw it too."

I sent him a silent *Thank you.*

Mr. Darning flicked Ben a look and he shut up. "Brianne, was it a real spider or a plastic one?"

I suddenly saw where Mr. Darning was going with this and suppressed a sigh of relief. I was tempted to tell him that someone had dropped an ugly plastic spider down my back, but I restrained myself. "It was a real spider. I'm sorry. I know it was...silly, but it startled me."

"That was quite a scream you gave over a spider." Mr. Darning didn't look like he believed me. "Rex Tremont sits behind you. He didn't do anything? Play a trick of some sort on you?"

I shook my head.

Mr. Darning sighed, but didn't press it. "Do you feel up to returning to your classes, or would you rather I phoned your parents?"

I thought first of the questions and curious stares I would face from my classmates, and then of the other set of questions I would get at home. It was an easy decision. I'd given my parents enough grief for a lifetime last year. I stood. "Class."

"Very well." Mr. Darning paused. "I trust this episode will not be repeated?"

I nodded emphatically. While the secretary nabbed Mr. Darning, I escaped out the door after Ben. "Thanks for backing me up," I said as we walked down the hall.

"No problem." Ben grinned. "That was the most interesting Science class we've had all year."

"Glad to be of service." I smiled back at him. I wanted to prolong the conversation so I said, "I can't believe Mr. Darning let me off so lightly." Mr. Darning had a razor-sharp tongue for students who stepped out of line.

"Mr. Darning's okay," Ben said.

"He's fair," I agreed. "But he sure doesn't cut anyone any slack." I gave a mock shiver.

"That's what I like about him," Ben said.

I blinked at this odd comment, but before I could ask him what he meant, we reached the classroom door. "Ready to go in?"

I straightened my shoulders. "Sure. Just do me a favour and let me know if I doze off again." Because Ben had been so nice, I wanted him to know a portion of the truth. "I think I must have had a nightmare."

Ben looked puzzled. "Usually when people fall asleep during class, they're resting their heads on their desks. You must have been really tired to fall asleep perched on one of those narrow stools."

"Guess so," I said. But a chill swept over me, because I hadn't been tired, and the idea that a nightmare could descend on me without warning at any time scared me worse than a dozen spiders.

chapter two

By noon the story of me screaming was all over school. Whenever I walked into a room, everyone stopped and stared at me. I felt like a freak.

It reminded me of the two awful months I'd spent being treated as walking leper in Edmonton. I told myself that this wasn't anywhere near as bad. All I'd done this time, really, was embarrass myself.

The last time I'd tried to use the knowledge my true dreams gave me to help solve a crime I'd ended up accused of the crime myself. Thinking about the unholy mess I'd made of my life last year—which had ended with our whole family being uprooted to Grantmere—made me feel sick to my stomach. With determination, I pushed the memory aside. I never wanted to think about that time in my life again.

I avoided the group of girls I usually had lunch with and sat by myself. I kept my head down and did homework between bites. That way I could pretend I didn't hear people talking about me.

A few people asked me outright what had happened. I told them that I'd been startled by a spider and fallen off my stool.

By the end of the day people were calling me "Miss Muffet."

I knew my sister, Suzy, had heard about what happened the minute we stepped off the bus. She wouldn't speak to me. Most days she talked my ear off, complaining about school and filling me in on the latest gossip. Today she just trudged along, shooting me accusing glances out of flashing blue eyes.

Boys might tell Suzy she was beautiful when she was angry, but in my opinion her blonde curls and bow-shaped mouth made her look like a pouty child when she frowned.

Although our eight-year-old sister, Lissa, still went to the elementary school she rode the same school bus that Suzy and I did. She took one look at the two of us and ran ahead, brown braids flying.

I didn't try to start a conversation. I was only a year older than Suzy, but she was a lot more impatient than I was. If I kept quiet, she'd give in and talk.

It worked.

"How could you do this to me *again*?" Suzy asked after only a minute had passed

"Do what?" I asked, not looking at her.

"You know what. All day long people kept looking at me funny and asking me questions about my flake of a sister. Did I know why you had screamed? Had you told me what happened?"

"I'm sorry *my* rotten day embarrassed *you*," I said with heavy sarcasm.

"You may not be trying to fit in, but I am. I was just starting to make real friends," Suzy wailed.

"I didn't want to move either." I snapped at her, but really I felt guilty. It was my fault Suzy had had to move to a new school last September and leave her old friends behind. "I wanted to stick it out. Moving was Mom and Dad's idea." Which was true and not true. I had been willing to stick it out, but, oh, the *relief* I'd felt at having the decision taken out of my hands.

And now my true dreams were starting up again. If I wasn't careful, I could end up back in the same position I'd been in at our last school. Shunned.

"I don't know what *you're* complaining about," I told Suzy. "You're not the one they're calling Miss Muffet."

"Are they really?" Suzy stopped dead.

"Yes." I glared at her, daring her to laugh.

"Oh, Brianne! I'm sorry."

I looked at Suzy and saw that she was being sincere.

"So what really happened?" Her voice was gentler. "Was there a spider?"

A picture of the huge black widow spider flashed through my mind, and I shuddered. "Yes." I stared at the weeds on the side of the driveway with apparent fascination. "I had a dream."

Suzy sucked in a breath. She knew what that meant as well as I did. "Was it bad?"

I grimaced. "Have I ever screamed at spiders before?"

Suzy digested that in silence. "Brianne?" Her voice was almost inaudible. "Do me a favour, will you? Don't tell Mom and Dad." I looked at her in surprise, and she spoke rapidly. "Not yet anyway. Not until you know *for sure*. I mean, what if it's only a one-time thing? Maybe they'll go away on their own like they did last time."

"Yeah, sure." My voice was flat. And maybe pigs would become jet pilots. Suzy looked just as unconvinced as I felt.

All the same, I didn't tell our parents.

* ✳ *

I spent the evening studying ecosystems, preparing for Mr. Darning's surprise quiz. If my dream followed its usual pattern, it would happen for real tomorrow, and I might as well benefit from the dream. I'd already paid the price.

There had been one plus to the whole experience. I remembered Ben's warm touch, and his concern. Had he just been being nice, or did he like me? Last year I would have been giddy and hopeful that he did, but last year I was a different Brianne.

Whether or not Ben liked me, he had been kind. Kindness was something I had a new appreciation for, and I found myself wishing I could do something nice for him.

My breath caught as I realized there was something I *could* do. I could warn him about the test.

My gut screamed that that was a bad idea—telling people about my dreams was what had gotten me into trouble last year—but I ignored it. As long as I contacted Ben anonymously, what could it hurt?

I looked up his phone number, started to dial on the second phone in Suzy's and my room, then hung up and dialed again on our for-road-trips-only cellphone. I knew from previous experience that the cell's number was blocked and wouldn't show up on Caller I.D.

I pinched my nose together with one hand. Suzy and I had discovered as kids that, while a dishcloth over the mouthpiece did little to disguise a person's voice, everyone sounded the same when they talked through their nose.

Two rings and a male voice answered the phone. "Hello?"

"Hi, may I speak to Ben please?" I said, even though I was pretty sure it was him. He might have a brother or something.

"Speaking," Ben said.

I hurried into speech. "Hi, Ben. Listen, I forgot to tell you, there's going to be a science test tomorrow."

"Tomorrow? I don't remember anything about a test," Ben said in such a way I knew he hadn't recognized my voice yet.

"I told you," I repeated nasally, "I forgot to tell you."

"Who is this anyway?" Ben sounded suspicious. "Is this some kind of joke?"

"Don't forget to study. Bye." I hung up and stared at the phone, half expecting Ben to ring back saying he had recognized my voice, and what on earth was I talking about? But the phone kept silent, and after a while I went to study some more myself.

I dreaded going to sleep that night, putting it off as long as I could. Suzy was already asleep and mumbling about her own dreams when I lay down. The faint sound of her breathing should have comforted me, but it didn't. Sleep was the enemy now.

Still, sitting here in the dark wasn't doing me any good. All I could do was cross my fingers and try not to dream.

Growing up, I'd had true dreams only very sporadically, twice a year at the most, until last spring when the trouble started. Then they'd suddenly become relentless night-after-night visits to hell—which had stopped as suddenly as a guillotine coming down after Aunt Elise died.

There was absolutely no reason why I should have a true dream tonight, I thought fiercely. None. I didn't dream that night, but instead of putting me in a good mood the next morning, I felt uneasy. My nerves tightened as I approached Science class—and the test that was to come. Part of me was hoping there wouldn't be a test, that yesterday's dream stayed just a dream. But the cynical part of me knew the dream had been real.

Ben smiled at me when I came into the lab, the only person to do so. "Hi. Study hard?"

Mr. Darning's entrance spared me replying. He immediately started going over the last chapter on ecosystems. Ben looked towards the front, a faint frown on his face. I winced. It was a good thing I hadn't identified myself over the phone or he would be ready to wring my neck.

Ten minutes later Rex Tremont sauntered into class. Anyone else would have slunk in, but Rex possessed the arrogance to match his outrageous good looks. He had white-blond hair, electric blue eyes, gym-club shoulders, and expensive clothes. I'd never seen a single pimple on his face. Sometimes I doubted that Rex was even human.

Rex dragged a stool over to sit by his friends in the row behind me. He flashed a smile at Mr. Darning, who was waiting for the interruption to end, arms crossed. "Sorry I'm late," Rex said.

Mr. Darning didn't look impressed. He had a stare that could freeze rubbing alcohol. "What time is it?" he asked Rex.

"Ten after nine," Rex said.

"Then you *do* own a watch?" Mr. Darning asked.

"Yes."

"Good. Try to learn how to use it before next class."

The put-down would have reduced me to blushes for the rest of the period. Not Rex. He just went on as usual.

A few minutes later, Rex whispered something that cracked up three of his friends, and Mr. Darning had enough. "All right, everyone close your books. I was going to put this off until you'd had a full day of review, but your behaviour shows me you feel ready to be tested today."

The class groaned in unison. Except for me. I felt the hairs rise on the back of my neck. It was happening. Now. Just as I'd dreamed.

The exam was taken in complete silence. Although the last question listed spider as one of the choices, I was relieved to notice that there was no spider illustration. As soon as I finished, I shoved my test to the far corner of my desk.

My gaze searched the classroom, colliding with Ben's; he too was finished early. Puzzlement showed on his face, and his blue eyes narrowed when he saw my face down test. Uh-oh, mistake. I jerked my gaze away.

Since the quiz only had twenty multiple-choice questions, we had time to mark the test during class. I did almost too well, pulling off a ninety-five percent.

The noon bell rang, and I saw with mixed feelings that Ben was waiting for me at the door. As much as I liked Ben, I didn't want him to find out that I was the one who had phoned him.

"So." Ben smiled at me. "How'd you do on the test?"

"All right. How about you?"

His mouth opened, but a voice behind me interrupted. "All right?" Rex asked. "Aren't you the modest one. You got ninety-five percent." He'd been sitting behind me and had corrected my paper. "Don't you know enough to brag about your good grades and save the put-downs for the bad ones?"

"No," I replied, my nerves on edge. "I guess I don't."

"Well, Ben here can tell you. Patrick says he got a ninety." Rex's eyes gleamed.

"And what did you get?" I asked Rex, trying to embarrass him into buzzing off. Rex's attitude towards Science and school in general was notoriously uncaring. He might have the face of a blond angel, but he wasn't one.

But Rex just smiled, showing off perfect white teeth. "Oh, I got eighty percent."

Ben's face looked thoughtful. "Well, I guess that makes us brains. Just about everyone else I talked to bombed."

Rex flashed another dazzling smile. "No such thing. I got an advance warning of the test, by anonymous phone call, no less."

Ben did a double-take, and I jerked, as if I'd been stung. How could Rex have gotten advanced warning about the test? I hadn't phoned Rex!

Ben recovered first. "A phone call? Was it from someone with a nasal voice?"

Rex nodded. "Yup. Why, did you get one too?" He cocked an eyebrow.

"Uh-huh." Ben turned to me. "How about you, Brianne?"

"Yy-yes." I choked over the lie, still staring at Rex in disbelief.

"That's strange," Ben said.

I nodded agreement. He didn't know the half of it!

"I wonder how the caller knew about the test?" Ben continued. "Mr. Darning said he was going to put it off, so in a sense, even he didn't know."

"Weird," I muttered since it seemed to be expected of me.

Rex shrugged. "Who cares? I'm just grateful they phoned me." He called out to somebody down the hall and jogged off. I stared after him, a cold lump settling in my stomach. I wasn't the only one lying about a phone call. But how had Rex found out?

"Brianne." Ben tried to regain my attention. "Are you doing anything Friday night?"

I blinked. As his words sank in, my heart began to pound. "Nothing special," I said.

"I was thinking about going to the movies," Ben said. "Would you like to go with me?"

My smile nearly split my face. "Yes. I'd like that a lot."

"Good." Ben grinned back, and the mess about the phone calls slipped away like water.

We ate lunch together. I could feel people staring at me again, but this time I didn't mind. This time they were staring at the two of us, not at Miss Muffet.

"If I had known screaming could get me noticed by Ben Harper, I would have shrieked my head off," I overheard one girl whisper.

My liking for Ben grew all through lunch. I liked his sense of humour. I liked his smile. I liked the way his dark brown hair fell over his forehead. And his eyes...I had to face it. I just plain liked him.

Ben was also easy to talk to. “So where did you live before moving to the huge metropolis of Grantmere?” he asked.

I laughed. Grantmere had a population of just over two thousand; the town was located close to the foothills of the Rockies and had mining roots, although these days most people made a living either logging or in the oil and gas industry. “In the huge metropolis of Edmonton, actually. But we lived in a small town before that, so don’t go thinking I’m a city girl.”

“Why did you move?”

I hesitated for a moment, and then told him part of the truth. “My Aunt Elise died, and Mom inherited her house. So when a forest technologist position came up out here my dad applied. He got it.”

Ben frowned. “Elise? Do you mean Elise Bessette, the writer?”

“Yes. Did you know her?”

“Not really. Just to recognize on the street. She was Grantmere’s claim to fame, you know, our resident best-selling author. I read one of her books once, from the library. *I Am Ghost.* Very scary.”

“That’s one of my favourites,” I said. We talked about scary books and then scary movies for the rest of the noon hour.

Except for the rare moments when I wondered just how Rex had gotten that phone call, I spent the rest of the day in a very good mood.

An odd thing happened on the bus ride home. Hayley Czernick skipped forward a couple of rows and sat beside me. “Hi.”

"Hi," I said back, perplexed. Hayley was in my grade, a pretty girl with a rather melodramatic air. She had straight ashy blonde hair, colourless lashes and liked to wear funky black hats. She'd always been friendly enough, but had never made any effort to talk to me before.

"I thought you and I should talk," she said in a dramatic whisper.

About what? I wondered.

Hayley filled me in. "I know there have been some rumours about Ben and me, and I wanted you to know that they just aren't true. Ben and I are friends, nothing more."

"Uh, good," I said, but inside I felt a sinking sensation. What rumours?

"Ben's a good guy," Hayley said, her expression earnest. "He deserves to be happy. I think you'll be good for him."

"Thanks," I said cautiously. I still didn't have a clue why Hayley had felt the need to tell me that she wasn't interested in Ben.

"He needs to get out more." Hayley lowered her voice again. "I was really worried about Ben for a while. He was so...fragile."

I stared. Fragile? Ben? Ben was solid all the way through. Anyone with eyes could see that.

"Anyhow, I just wanted to let you know that I'm glad the two of you are dating," Hayley finished in a rush. She stood up and slung her backpack over her shoulder; the bus had pulled to a stop in front of her driveway.

Hayley lived only a quarter mile down the road from our acreage, and I was still confused when my turn came to get off the bus a minute later.

"What did she want?" Suzy asked as we started to walk down the driveway.

"I'm not sure," I said. "She wanted to let me know that she was glad Ben asked me out."

Suzy whooped. "He did?" She dropped her bag, grabbed my shoulders and spun me into a silly dance. I was laughing when she finished.

"Ben Harper, huh? He's very cute."

"Yes," I agreed.

"So?" she demanded. "Fill me in on all the details!"

"What details?" I stalled, but I couldn't stop smiling.

"What details, she asks!" Suzy punched me in the shoulder. "When are you going out? How did he ask you? How long has he been interested in you?"

"He asked me to the movies Friday night. It's actually the dream's fault," I said. "I fell off my stool, and Ben helped me up." I told Suzy all about it.

She listened with a thoughtful frown. "Nah, it wasn't the screaming. I bet he liked you before. Was he sitting beside you in class?"

"No," I said wistfully. Guys probably schemed to sit by Suzy all the time. "He was a couple of seats over in the next row."

"Even better. That means he had to rush over to be there when you opened your eyes. He totally likes you. And didn't you say he knew you didn't have your head down on your desk? He must have been watching you."

I wasn't as sure, but the possibility gave me a warm feeling. "So what about you?" I teased Suzy. "Who's the lucky guy this week?" Every time we talked she had a crush on someone new.

She hesitated. "If I tell you, I'm afraid I'll jinx it. I really like him, but I'm not sure if he's interested in me or if he just likes to flirt."

"What did he say?" I asked, curious.

"We were standing around outside school, and he asked if I was new in town. I said, Sort of, we've been here since September, and he snapped his fingers and said, Hey, I bet you're Brianne Foster's sister—Brianne's *pretty* little sister. I said that I was and told him my name, and he asked if it was Suzy or Susie, Susan or Suzanne, or Suz."

"Definitely flirting," I agreed. "So what does he look like? Give me a hint."

Suzy smiled secretively, but didn't tell me his name.

chapter three

I didn't dream that night, and it was only when I approached Science again the next morning that my worries returned. The test part of my dream had come true, but I was still puzzled by the spider.

Ben came over to talk before class and told me a joke. I smiled, but kept my eyes on the door, watching for Rex. The more I thought about his test mark and the phone call he claimed to have received, the uneasier I became.

"I think I know where you live," Ben said. "An acreage on the north side of town, right? Two lefts and then the third house on the right?"

"Yes. How'd you know?" I asked, curious.

"You said it was your aunt's house. I know she lived next door to Czernick's."

Hayley. His answer didn't make me happy.

Just then Mr. Darning came in, and Ben slipped back to his own stool. Class began, and this time, instead of showing up late, Rex didn't show up at all.

I spent most of the school day mentally reviewing and rejecting half the clothes in my closet. Everything I had seemed old and boring. I hadn't bought new clothes in forever. Maybe there was something in Suzy's closet I could borrow.

I broached the subject with Suzy while we walked down the driveway, but she was grinning from ear to ear and didn't hear a word I said. Lissa and I lagged behind, staring at our sister.

"What's with her?" Lissa quirked her thin eyebrows in a comical expression of puzzlement.

I shrugged. "Beats me."

Suzy's mood had undergone a drastic change by the time we reached the house. She had a sullen expression, and was listening to Mom lecture her. "...and furthermore, you're going to make up for skipping class by staying home all weekend."

"But Mom!" Suzy looked horrified. "I have a date tonight. I can't cancel out now."

Mom remained inflexible. "You can and you will."

Suzy looked near tears. "I don't see why you're so upset. Other kids skip class all the time."

"Not my kids." Mom's lips thinned.

"But it's not as if I missed anything important," Suzy said. "I knew all we were going to be doing today was working on our reports, and I finished mine last class. Please can I go?"

I was pretty sure I knew the answer to that, so I took Lissa by the shoulders and steered her into the living room. Suzy would be angry about having to stay home tonight; she didn't need me rubbing it in by asking to borrow some clothes for my date. I would just have to settle for my own dull clothes. Maybe my red striped T-shirt...

I wondered why she had skipped out, but postponed such thinking until after I'd washed and styled my hair. It was so short that there wasn't much to it.

A few months ago, my hair had been waist-length. My reflection still took me by surprise some days. It had been my mom's idea to get it cut, saying I should get a "new look for a new town," but I'd known that wasn't the true reason. The short hair acted as something of a disguise, made it less likely someone would recognize me from last year's notoriety.

I'd let Mom talk me into the haircut because I'd wanted a new look for the new Brianne: older, wiser, and stronger than last year's model.

I was ready half an hour before Ben was supposed to pick me up. I'd developed a bumper crop of nerves by the time the doorbell rang at 7:25 PM. I ran to answer it, but Lissa beat me to it. She said, "Hello Ben," in her most grown-up voice and asked him in.

"Hi." I grinned at him, noting the way his dark hair curled around his ears. "This is my sister, Lissa." For a second, I wondered how Lissa had known Ben's name, but just then Mom came in from the kitchen, wiping her hands on a dish towel. "And this is my mom. Mom, this is Ben Harper."

"Nice to meet you," Mom said.

"You, too, Mrs. Foster." Ben shook her hand.

While I put on my coat, Mom asked him a few questions. What movie were we going to go see? What time would he have me home by? What were his parents' names?

I blushed when she asked him if he had any speeding tickets. "Mom!"

"Zero." Ben met her gaze dead on. "I'm a very safe driver."

Mom nodded, as if satisfied.

"We have to go now or we'll be late." I pulled Ben out the door before she could come up with any more embarrassing questions. "Sorry about that."

"Don't worry about it. More mothers should think twice about who they let drive their kids."

The movie was fun, a science fiction spoof, and Ben turned out to share my liking for red licorice.

Afterward, a crowd of high school kids gathered on the street outside the theatre, and Ben and I stood there for a while, talking. His arm was around my waist, and I was up where the stars hung in the sky.

Or at least I was until I happened to glance over and recognize Rex's midnight blue sports car. He had his window rolled down, talking to some kids. There was another blonde head beside him in the car, talking and laughing, too. My eyes nearly bugged out: it was Suzy.

Rex turned and looked straight at me. He smiled, and I had the funniest feeling he had known I was watching. That he wanted me to see Suzy and him together.

Suzy turned, laughing. Then she saw me, and the sight wiped the smile off her face. She said something to Rex, and he gave a mocking little wave before pulling away from the curb and roaring down the street. I was left staring, my heart pounding. I liked this less and less. What was going on?

"Idiot," Ben said.

"What?" I asked, startled.

"Rex. The way he drives he's going to get in an accident one day. If he hasn't already." Ben's face was grim.

A boy whose name I couldn't remember—Pat? Patrick?—invited us to a party. "You're coming, right Ben?" he said, his voice a shade too hearty. "Of course, you are, you're a party dude." He punched Ben's shoulder.

"We'll think about it," Ben said, non-committal. We said our goodbyes, then walked to where we'd parked Ben's pickup. The motor started with a rusty growl; Ben let it idle a moment. "So do you want to go to the party?"

"We could," I said, more because I didn't want the night to end than because I wanted to go to a party.

"We can go if you want to," Ben said. He didn't sound very enthused.

"Do you want to go?" I asked him.

Ben grimaced. "No. I'm not a 'party dude.'"

"Me either," I confessed.

"I have an idea," Ben said. "Let's go to the park." He put the truck in gear, while I blinked.

My stomach jumped with nerves. Did he want to make out? I wanted to kiss him, but this was just our first date—

We arrived at the tiny park, and Ben immediately opened his door and hopped out.

Not sure whether to be relieved or disappointed, I followed, and Ben took my hand. "Come on." The further we went into the park, the darker it got. I stumbled once over a rock, and Ben steadied me. Soon my eyes adjusted, and I saw a small playground ahead.

We went on the swings. "Look at the stars," Ben said as we swung side by side.

I held tight to the chains and leaned way back. "Wow." They were very bright that night. I could see the Big Dipper, Orion and Cassiopeia. Ben tried to show me where the Pole Star was, but I couldn't find it. "The stars are moving too fast," I complained.

Ben laughed at me. "You're barely moving." He started to pump his legs, making his swing go higher and higher. Our swings went out of synch, and I pumped harder, trying to catch him, but couldn't. Breathless, I gave up and leaned back, looking up as the swing made its long arc. The stars smeared by in a dizzying rush.

When I got too dizzy, we got off and climbed a net of chains going up one side of the jungle gym. I crossed a swaying bridge of tires, then turned and couldn't find Ben.

"Ben?" I suddenly became aware of just how dark it was. "Ben?" I crossed back over the bridge, searching in vain. I scrambled down a ladder, every horror movie I'd ever seen running through my head.

I almost jumped out of my skin when Ben touched my shoulder from behind. He was grinning. I narrowed my eyes at him. "Now you're in for it," I told him.

"Only if you catch me." He started running, and I pursued, chasing him up ladders and through plastic tunnels. My arms weren't strong enough to follow him hand-over-hand on the monkey bars, and I had to jump to the ground and find another set of steps back up. He kept ahead with ease, and I remembered that he played on the school basketball team. I was out of breath and grateful when he took a spiral slide down. I followed—and ran into him at the bottom.

"Umph." I laughed as I smacked into him.

But it seemed that had been Ben's intention all along, because his arms went around me then, and he kissed me. His lips were soft and warm.

"That was nice," I murmured, when he lifted his head a moment later, gazing starry-eyed at his face.

"Yeah?" A dimple kicked out in Ben's chin. And he kissed me again.

Then it was time to go to make my curfew. I felt shy once we were back in Ben's old pickup, not sure if I should cuddle up to him or sit on the other side of the gearshift. He put on his seat belt, so I sat by the window and pulled the shoulder strap across my body.

When the pickup rolled to a stop in front of my house, I sat a moment longer, hoping Ben would ask me out again.

But Ben's face was serious, almost brooding, as he looked at the house. "Do you miss her?" he asked suddenly. "Your aunt?"

"Yes." I hesitated. "I didn't get to see her that much, but we were buds." I had an interest in writing, but even before that the two of us had had a bond.

Which was why it had hurt so much that I'd been unable to attend her funeral. I would never forgive Detective Reuter for that.

"What was she like?" Ben turned his head toward me, and I could no longer make out his expression.

"She was really cool. Very creative, never boring. She travelled a lot and had been to a lot of neat places." I bit my lip, fighting tears. Most of the time I could pretend Aunt Elise was away on a trip somewhere. I didn't like to think about her being dead. "She always sent us souvenirs, different stuff, not just postcards and knick-knacks."

Ben put his hand over mine and squeezed. "She sounds nice."

I thought he was going to say something else, but just then the porch light came on. I choked out a laugh. "I think that's a hint." I opened the door before Mom went so far as to come outside and stand on the step. "Bye."

"Bye, Brianne," Ben said, his voice warm. "I'll call you tomorrow, okay?"

"Okay," I said, but it was more than okay, it was great. I watched him drive out of sight, said goodnight to Mom, and floated down the hall to my room.

Suzy was already in bed with her eyes closed, though I rather doubted she was asleep. The memory of her in Rex's car flooded back.

"Suzy?" I stood there for a moment, but she kept still, her breathing a little too deep to be believable. "Give it up," I told her. "I know you're awake."

Silence. Suzy always was stubborn.

"I'm not going to tell Mom and Dad. Or at least I won't if you talk to me. Come on," I coaxed. "I'll tell you about my date if you'll tell me about yours."

Suzy sat up so fast she might have been on springs. She didn't look the least bit sleepy. "It was so great! I had the best time."

My heart sank. I didn't like Rex, and I didn't trust him, and there was something very weird going on with him. I'd been hoping his true colours had shown through and Suzy didn't like him anymore.

However, I was smart enough not to say so. "You couldn't have had *the* best time," I said, "because I had the best time with Ben."

She giggled. "Yeah, where have you been? The movie finished an hour ago."

So I told her about the playground and watching the stars and the kiss at the bottom of the slide. It felt pleasant. I didn't have any real friends yet in Grantmere, but the absolute only good thing that had come out of last year's fiasco was that Suzy and I had grown closer. Friends as well as sisters.

"So can you top that?" I asked.

"Yours was more romantic," she conceded. "But mine was more fun." She paused for effect. "Rex let me drive his car."

"A brave man." In spite of myself, I was impressed. Suzy, at sixteen, had just acquired her license, and most guys were reluctant to lose control over their wheels, no matter how rattletrap. That Rex had let her drive his flashy blue sports car implied a lot of trust on his part.

"We went out on the highway, put the top down and opened it up. It was like flying." Suzy's eyes shone.

I liked the convenience of being able to drive and not having to depend on Mom and Dad for rides. Suzy liked the physical driving, whipping along curves.

"Sounds like a good way to get bugs in your hair," I said.

Suzy stuck out her tongue at me.

"How far did you go?"

"For miles. All the way to the intersection with the Yellowhead Highway." She talked for ten minutes about how cool Rex was and how much fun.

I listened to her until she ran out of steam. "Let me ask you one question. Was it his idea for you to sneak out?"

Suzy tossed back her hair. "No. It was mine."

I bet Rex hadn't objected much. "And skipping class this morning, was that your idea, too?"

Suzy bit her lip. "It was my idea to tag along. I saw Rex in the parking lot with his skateboard just before the bell rang. He said that Mr. Darning always taught from the textbook, and he could read the chapter later. I told him I had a spare, and he invited me along." Suzy paused. "I won't do it again, if that's what you're worried about. Mom would ground me for a month."

"Okay." I accepted her promise, and she started to talk about how they'd gone to the skateboard park and taken turns practicing on Rex's skateboard.

I listened, but by the time she was done singing Rex's praises—"his technique needs some work, but he's not afraid to try"—a lot of my good mood had been spoiled.

I tossed around in bed waiting for sleep to come. As always my mind turned to the dreams. What had the spider dream meant? And above all, why now? It had taken me a year to straighten out from last time, and now the dreams were starting up again. It wasn't fair.

I lay stiffly on my mattress and tried to calm down. The dream had just been a one-time thing, I assured myself. I hadn't dreamed last night, and I wouldn't tonight.

But, of course, it wasn't a one-time thing.

In the hollowness of the night, I dreamed that I walked with a dead woman.

Aunt Elise looked much as she had in life. Her thick brown hair was pulled back in an untidy knot, and she wore a white nightgown. Her eyes were dark and sad, holding none of their usual humour. Maybe they had always been sad, and I hadn't seen it.

She glided in front of me, leading the way down an endless hallway. Tendrils of mist curled around her bare feet although we were indoors.

I hurried after her, preferring the company of a ghost to being alone in this strange place. "What is it?" I asked her. "What do you want to show me?"

She didn't answer, only moved on. The featureless hallway was broken suddenly by a skull set high in a glass display case. I paused before it and read the small plaque identifying it as the skull of a timber wolf.

Aunt Elise didn't slow down, and I hurried after her, never quite able to catch up. I was desperate to keep her in sight, terrified that the mist would swallow her and I would be alone. We passed a cluster of three other display cases. Inside grinned more skulls: a hyena, a coyote and an Australian wild dog.

A long interval of hallway passed before we reached another lupine skull, a large monstrosity labelled Dire Wolf, a creature that had lived during the last Ice Age. I shuddered when I looked at it.

Aunt Elise looked back over her shoulder. Her lips didn't move, but I heard her voice. *There are worse things than wolves.*

We walked farther, and I had the sudden perception that as we went down the hall, we were going back in time. The skulls became fossils, gray and brittle, with portions missing and other bits wired together.

The intervals between skulls got longer and longer, so that it seemed we had walked for miles when the hallway finally dead-ended. A large glass case waited for us. As I got closer, I saw that it contained a full skeleton, not just a head. Goosebumps dimpled my flesh as I looked at it. Its teeth grinned horribly, and its empty eye sockets stared.

I had the crazy feeling that it could see me. That in a moment the head would turn, and it would lunge at me, breaking the glass.

"What is it?" I asked Aunt Elise, although the brass nameplate said *Wulfdraigle.*

Again, her lips didn't move, but I heard her speech clearly inside my head. "*The wulfdraigles are watching...*" She repeated the last words she'd ever said to me and vanished.

I woke up very cold and afraid to move. I listened to Suzy's even breathing across the room and tried not to wake her with my own gasps. It was just a dream, I told myself, that's all. And dreams were distorted. After all, following my black widow dream there hadn't been a spider diagram, and I hadn't flunked the test.

When my bedroom door was pushed open, I came very near to screaming and was quite glad I hadn't when I saw who it was. Lissa. Her long brown hair was tousled, and she looked sleepy. She climbed into my lap, put her thin arms around my neck and hugged me. "Lissa," I whispered, "What are you doing up?"

She giggled, her elf smile popping up. "S'okay, Brianne. I won't let them hurt you. Not ever."

A chill ran up my spine. "Won't let who hurt me?" My voice was sharp. "Lissa?" I shook her, but her eyes stayed closed. The terror of the dream returned. How had Lissa known I was even awake, much less in need of company?

chapter four

The wulfdraigles are watching. All the next morning, I kept turning Aunt Elise's words over in my head. What had she meant? There were no such creatures as wulfdraigles. Or were there?

I decided to ask Mom about it. Aunt Elise had been her sister; maybe she knew what it meant. She was dusting when I found her, singing along to the Beatles and dancing in shorts and a tank top.

It made me feel guilty to watch Mom cleaning the house. Mom had a high-powered personality. She attacked everything she did with enthusiasm. When I was in elementary school, my mom was always the one who baked special cakes for class parties, volunteered in the school library, was a member of the parent's association and took university courses by correspondence or distance learning. When Lissa started school three years ago, Mom had finally had a chance to go back into the workforce. We'd moved to Edmonton, Dad had commuted to his old job in Westlock, and Mom had started working for Alberta Education. She'd just received a promotion when my dreams caused all the trouble. Her career had gone back on hold, and the whole family had moved to Grantmere—supposedly so Mom could decide what to do with Aunt Elise's house, but really because of me.

Her talents were wasted on housekeeping.

"Mom?" I said. She turned around, holding a vase as she dusted. "What are the wulfdraigles?"

Crash! The vase slipped from her fingers and splintered on the floor.

"Don't move." Mom gingerly picked her way over to the hall closet to get the broom and dustpan. It wasn't until the glass was all swept up and deposited in the trash that she turned and looked at me again. "Now then, what were you saying?"

I repeated my question, adding, "I remember Aunt Elise mentioning them."

"The wulfdraigles?" Mom shrugged. "Sorry, I don't remember ever hearing of them before." She went back to dusting, and I left, uneasy. Because her hands had been shaking. Because I was almost positive she was lying.

Ben's call that afternoon was a welcome distraction. The sound of his voice sent a thrill through me. "Brianne?"

"Yes, it's me."

"Listen, I've been invited to a party this afternoon. Last night when I said I wasn't a party dude, I didn't mean I never went to parties," Ben said awkwardly. "I—"

"I knew what you meant," I assured him. "You just weren't in the mood to be around a lot of people last night. I wasn't either."

"So...what about today? Want to come?"

"Yes," I said, not caring if I sounded too eager. I wanted to see Ben. "Hang on while I ask if it's okay." I covered the receiver and yelled for Mom. She cleared it, and I switched back to Ben. "I can come."

"Great." Ben's voice was warm. "I'll pick you up in say—" he paused as if to consult his watch, "—half an hour. Okay?"

"Okay, bye." I waited for the click at the end of the line, and after a moment realized Ben was doing the same thing. We both laughed and hung up.

After a look at the thermometer, I changed into a clean pair of denim shorts and a yellow T-shirt. The day was another scorcher. Nice for parties, but not so good for the already tinder-dry forests. There were 208 fires burning in Alberta and this was only the beginning of June. Some days we could smell smoke from the Douglas Hills fire, but the wind must have been blowing the right direction today because the air was perfectly clear.

While I waited for Ben to arrive, I went into the kitchen to get myself a glass of juice and found Mom and Lissa arguing. Lissa was mad at Mom for disposing of a spider web while she was dusting. "I was saving that spider!" she said, on the verge of tears.

Mom was sympathetic but practical. "I don't like spider webs in the house, Lissa. If you wanted a spider, you should have let me know. I would have given you a jar with air holes to keep it in."

"Did you kill it?" Lissa asked.

"No, I took it outside," Mom said. "Spiders eat mosquitoes and flies, remember? They're good critters."

"I don't like them," Lissa said.

Mom lost patience. “Then what did you want one for? Do you have a school project?”

“No. I wanted to step on it, so it would rain.” Forlorn, Lissa left the kitchen.

I stared after her. Step-on-a-spider was a game I’d played myself at age eight, but Lissa playing it made me uneasy. It was too close to my dream.

I went out to meet Ben when he drove up and climbed in the front seat beside him. “Hi, are you—” He stopped suddenly and craned his neck around. “Why did your sister just climb into the back of my truck?”

I turned around and sure enough there was Suzy, lying flat on the bed of the pickup. She signaled frantically for us to go.

“What do you want me to do?” Ben asked.

I thought about it. Suzy was obviously trying to sneak off to see Rex again. “Drive a little ways down the road, then stop.”

Ben did so without another word, driving carefully so as to avoid the road’s many potholes. As soon as he parked on the side of the road, Suzy climbed out of the back and headed for the passenger door. She was smiling.

I rolled down the window, but didn’t unlock it. “What are you doing?”

“What do you think?” Suzy rolled her eyes. “I want a ride to Rex’s party.”

The party was at Rex’s house? Crap.

“Well, you can’t come with us,” I snapped. “If you do, Mom will ground both of us.”

“I’ll tell her I got a ride with someone else,” Suzy wheedled.

No way was I going to help her see Rex. "No." I leaned close and whispered, "How'd you like it if I horned in on *your* date?"

"But—"

"Goodbye." I heartlessly rolled up the window, ignoring the stormy look on Suzy's face. Ben raised an eyebrow. "Let's go," I told him.

"Okay." Ben put the pickup back in gear.

Fifteen minutes later we arrived at Rex's house—though house didn't seem like the right word. Estate, more like. The place had gates. Genuine iron gates with the name *Huxton* scrolled in them. I frowned. "I thought Rex's last name was Tremont."

"It is. Huxton is the name of his guardian. Rex came to live with him about four or five years ago."

Before I could ask why Rex had a guardian, we were through the gates, and there were other things to look at.

"I don't believe it!" I turned incredulous eyes to Ben. "All this in Grantmere?" Rich hockey players might live like this in Edmonton, but the residence was way out of place in Grantmere.

The grounds were bright green, attesting to constant watering in the drought. I glimpsed a miniature golf course and a croquet course. The house was huge and white. Long tables on the veranda were heaped with junk food and staffed by uniformed caterers.

"I don't believe it," I repeated, while extricating myself from the pickup where my bare legs had stuck to the seat. As soon as I opened my door, a blast of music hit us, almost deafening me.

Instead of Grantmere's usual country and western fare, rock music poured out on the front lawn from at least four giant speakers. The extreme heat had called for desperate measures—water fights—complete with water machine guns and water balloons. The amount of water used rather appalled me—the Douglas Hills fire wasn't that far away from Grantmere and the forest was bone-dry—but I soon calmed down. The town had a whole big reservoir built specifically for the demands of a dry summer. People laughed and screamed everywhere, the party in full swing. Ben pulled me forward, and we joined in.

I had just gotten soaked and was laughing helplessly at Ben, who was getting the same treatment, when the person behind me whispered, "The wulfdraigles are watching," near my ear. I jumped and swivelled my head so fast the bones in my neck cracked.

I got hosed for my pains, but I just stood there and let the water spray all over me, my heart beating painfully fast.

I don't know what I expected, but all I saw was Tillie Gerard, a classmate of Suzy's, holding a hose and killing herself laughing. "Oh Brianne," she giggled, "You should see your face!"

My own laughter had died, and I stared her down. "Did you say—that?" I could not quite bring myself to repeat the words.

Tillie pouted. "Of course I did. Though I must say," she smiled slyly, "I didn't expect quite such a reaction. What are wulfdraigles anyway?"

I ignored her question. If she didn't know what the wulfdraigles were, then how had she known to say it in the first place? I took a wild shot. "Who told you to say that to me?"

"Wouldn't *you* like to know?" Tillie asked.

I stared at her hard enough to crack glass. "Who, Tillie? Tell me."

Her gaze shifted under mine, over to a group of kids playing volleyball. "Oh look," she said in a fake, too-high voice. "There's Patrick. I must go talk to him."

"Not so fast." I grabbed her arm. "Not until you answer my question. Who? Who told you to say it?"

Her eyes flashed with irritation. "Rex, okay? Are you satisfied? Now lay off, Miss Muffet!"

I let go without another word, staring around blankly.

The speaker nearest me was suddenly jacked up another couple of notches right in the middle of a song I didn't know.

Be careful what you wish for, baby,
Be careful what you dream about,
It may all come true, in the twilight...

There, by the CD player, stood Rex. He looked straight at me, smiled in a way that probably turned Suzy's knees to jelly, and walked toward me. My instinct was to back away; I stood my ground with effort. I had never trusted Rex's angelic appearance. His blue eyes were just a little too blue, his teeth too white.

"Like the music, Brianne?" he asked, and my throat closed up. My mind screeched in alarm. He knew! Rex knew about my dreams. The knowledge was there in his eyes.

"Hi Rex." Ben came to stand at my shoulder. I positioned myself beside him gratefully. "Great party you have here."

"Glad you like it," Rex said, playing the host.

My mind worked furiously, even as I listened to them. There was a simple explanation for all this. There had to be. Rex must have recognized me from the newspaper photo taken last year and was taunting me. *But what about the wulfdraigles?* That had happened last night. How had he known about that?

Rex was looking at me intently, and I pressed my lips together in a line. He mustn't see how frightened I was.

"So," Ben said, "where's your guardian, Sir Jeremy? Away on a trip as usual?"

"He's home, but, trust me, you don't want to see him." Rex said with a strange smile.

"Oh, I don't know," Ben said. "I'm getting curious. This is the fifth time I've been to one of your parties, and I've never seen him. I'm beginning to suspect he's a ghost!"

"Only if ghosts wear bow ties and have long white mustaches," Rex said.

"No reason why they couldn't," Ben joked. "I'm just surprised he's home. My parents would never let me play music this loud. Does he like rock?"

"He hates it," Rex said casually. "That and teenagers are his two pet peeves. But don't worry about it." His blue eyes gleamed. "I can handle the old man."

I sensed a threat behind Rex's words.

"Talk to you guys later," Rex said, already moving away. "Say hi to your sister for me, Brianne." He tossed the last words over his shoulder.

I stared after him until Ben spoke, "Earth to Brianne, come in Brianne."

"Sorry." I smiled at him. We headed over to the buffet table, and I nibbled at some potato chips. There was a lot of joking and partying going on, but I couldn't get back into the spirit of things. The mention of the wulfdraigles and the playing of "Be Careful" had upset me more than I cared to admit. If it had been anyone else, I might have shrugged it off as coincidence, but not Rex. I didn't trust him. Not with anything, especially not Suzy.

Rex was playing with me, and I didn't like it. I was tired of Rex always knowing more than I did. Abruptly, I decided to go on the offensive. I told Ben I needed to use the washroom and brazenly set off for the Huxton mansion. I breezed past the caterers like I knew where I was going and started looking for Rex's bedroom. I knew it was unlikely that I would find any clues, but I couldn't stand to just do nothing.

I didn't have much time, so I didn't let myself stop and gawk at the paintings and the glass and the marble, but I wanted to. The Huxton mansion was a shining treasure trove.

It occurred to me that I would hate to live in a treasure trove. I saw lots of art, but few signs that a teenager lived in the house.

I glanced at my watch. I'd been inside for close to ten minutes already. One more hallway and I'd have to give up.

I opened doors and peeked in. I saw a sunroom and a billiard room and a library. I was about to close the library door again, when I saw three glass display cases containing skulls. The memory of last night's dream drew me inside. The first case held the skull of a timber wolf, the second a dire wolf. The third was listed as "unidentified," but I would have sworn it was the same wulfdraigle skull I'd dreamed of last night.

What did it mean?

I was still peering up at the skull when a small rustle grabbed my attention. I spun around and discovered I wasn't alone. Sir Jeremy was sitting in a wing-back chair in front of the fire. I was relieved to see that his eyes were closed. He gave another small snore—the same sound that had alerted me to his presence.

Sir Jeremy was wearing an old-fashioned suit and a green bow tie. His hair and mustaches were white and luxuriant, his face tanned, but his clothes looked too big for his body, as if he'd recently been ill.

The mystery of the skulls would have to wait. I started to tiptoe past, and his eyes opened. They were a muddy hazel and seemed befuddled.

It would have been rude to just leave the room, so I paused awkwardly. "Sorry to bother you," I whispered. "I got lost on my way to the bathroom."

He frowned. He probably had a hearing problem.

I raised my voice. "Can you tell me where the bathroom is?"

He kept scowling. "Who are you?"

"Brianne Foster. I'm a guest of Rex's. He's having a party," I added, in case Sir Jeremy's memory was also deficient.

"Rex." His lips thinned, and he looked like he wanted to spit.

I sensed a possible ally. "Are you upset with Rex?"

Before Sir Jeremy could reply, the library door opened partway. I saw the back of Rex's blond head. "She's probably outside looking for you," Rex told someone. "You should go back outside."

"I heard her voice in there," Ben said, and the door swung open. Ben crossed the room toward me. "Brianne. I've been looking for you."

Rex followed him, looking grim.

"I got lost trying to find the bathroom." I trotted out my lie. "I was just about to ask Sir Jeremy where one was."

Sir Jeremy was squinting at Ben. "Who're you?"

"Ben—"

Rex raised his voice suddenly, drowning out Ben's last name. He all but threw himself between Ben and Sir Jeremy. "And this is Sir Jeremy. He's not a ghost, after all, but he is very tired, so we should all leave him in peace now." He put an arm around both our shoulders and pulled us forward.

"It was nice to meet you, sir. I'm sorry if we disturbed you," Ben said over his shoulder.

"I don't believe in ghosts," Sir Jeremy said strongly. He rose to his feet.

Rex abandoned us and stood in front of his guardian. "There are no ghosts. Now why don't you sit back down and take your medicine?"

Sir Jeremy's eyes turned icy. "Don't you be giving me orders, boy. I'm the master of this house, and I say there are no ghosts." He stabbed his index finger at Ben. "That boy is alive!"

"Of course he is. His name is Ben," Rex said soothingly, then turned on Ben and me. "Get out of here!"

We went. I lingered at the door to see if I could overhear any more, but Ben looked at me curiously, and I gave up the attempt.

"Wow," Ben said, once we were outside. "Sounds like Sir Jeremy's a bit senile. Rex sure seemed protective of him.

I nodded, but privately I thought that Rex wasn't so much protecting Sir Jeremy as keeping him isolated. A senile old man, easily overruled by a stronger younger man. I wondered if Rex was even Sir Jeremy's true ward or if he was just living here, sponging off him. If Sir Jeremy had Alzheimer's, Rex could tell Sir Jeremy he was his grandson and Sir Jeremy wouldn't know not to believe him.

But those were big ifs. All I really knew was that there was something wrong with the relationship between Rex and Sir Jeremy.

chapter five

I took a deep breath. "Suzy, can I talk to you for a moment?" On the drive home from the party, I'd decided this was the next step, but I was dreading it.

In answer Suzy turned up the volume on the soap opera she taped. Guess she was still mad at me.

"Come on," I said, "I'll tell you about the party."

That captured her attention. She paused the tape. "Did you talk to Rex? Did he ask about me? He wasn't with anyone else, was he?"

"No," I said, startled. "He said to say hello to you."

Her face fell. "Nothing else?"

"We didn't talk about you," I said with more truth than tact.

Suzy's eyes flashed. "What did you talk about?"

"Look, Suzy, I know you like Rex, but I think there's something weird going on with him." I fumbled through an explanation of how Rex had known about the surprise quiz and what had happened at today's party. I knew I was blowing it when Suzy's expression of hostility didn't change.

"So you think I should break up with Rex because he got 80% on his Science test, and he likes the song 'Be Careful,'" Suzy said scornfully. "Yeah, I don't think so."

"Don't you get it? He knew about my dream," I said.

Suzy crossed her arms. "You told Ben Harper about your dream; you don't know how many people he phoned and told."

I was pretty sure Ben hadn't phoned anyone, but I could see I wouldn't convince Suzy. "And the wulfdraigles?"

She tilted her head. "You said Aunt Elise told you about them; it's probably some local legend. In any case, Tillie's the one who told you it was Rex, and I wouldn't trust Tillie to tell me if it was raining."

I opened my mouth to object, but she turned the TV back on and pointedly ignored me.

Before I could think of a comeback, the phone rang.

"It's Daddy!" Lissa shouted from the kitchen.

Dad was on the phone! Mom put him on speakerphone, and we took turns talking to him. Dad spoke to Lissa first, then Suzy, listening with real interest to each of us. Finally, it was my turn. "Well, Brianne? Anything new with you?" Underneath his light tone I sensed a worry that hadn't been there a year ago, and my dreams flooded back to me with awful clarity.

Suzy shot me a half-fierce, half-pleading look, and I told him about the 95% on my Science test and my date with Ben instead.

"And it's Ben, is it? Not Benjy?" Dad asked.

"No! Benjy's a dog's name," I said.

"Well, maybe this Ben is a dog," Dad teased me. "How do I know? I haven't met him. I'll have to ask your mother for the secret spy report." He continued in a similar vein for a few minutes.

"So, how's the firefighting going?" I asked.

"We held our ground today," Dad said. "We borrowed a couple of water bombers from B.C., Sikorsky Skycranes that can drop nine tonnes, and that really helped. They cooled down part of the fire enough for crew to move in with picks and shovels. There are thirty caterpillars clearing brush around town, making a firebreak. We should make good progress tonight. But the forecast tomorrow is for a cold front to move in, and if the winds pick up…." he trailed off.

If the wind picked up to more than 35 km/h, the fire crews wouldn't be able to hold the fire. And wind speeds could go as high as 80km/h.

"But hopefully the wind will shift and blow the fire back onto itself rather than toward Douglas Hills," Dad said.

He asked to talk to Mom next, and I relinquished the phone. I felt guilty about not telling him about my dream.

When Mom hung up, she looked at the time and winced. "I have to go. I have a Social Action committee meeting tonight. Can you make your own supper?"

"We'll be fine," Suzy said for all of us. But only minutes after Mom left I heard her talking a mile a minute on the phone. To Rex, I wondered?

I ruffled Lissa's fine brown hair, which was so like my own. "Looks like it's just you and me, kid." She giggled. "What do you want for supper?"

Lissa picked hot dogs, and I nuked them, ignoring the face Suzy pulled when she saw them on her plate. After supper,

Suzy staked out our bedroom, so I took my homework to the living room.

Lissa was there, sitting on the floor, a heavy dictionary spread across her lap. I knelt beside her. "What're you looking for? Maybe I can help."

Lissa's head came up, her eyes very wide. Her hands covered the page.

Warning bells went off in my head, but I ignored them, looking over her shoulder. "Is it the spelling you're having trouble with? What's the word?"

"It's two words," she corrected me. "Wolf draigles."

The skin on my face, arms, neck—everywhere—crawled. I stared at Lissa. "Where did you hear that? Did you hear me talking to Mom?"

"Yes, but I heard Aunt Elise say it first."

For a moment the breath stopped in my lungs—had Lissa dreamed of Aunt Elise, too?—until I realized she probably meant that she'd heard Aunt Elise say it while our aunt was still alive. "Do you remember what she said about them?"

"She said they were bad."

Which wasn't much help.

A crushing headache sent me to bed at nine o'clock. I evicted Suzy and lay down on the bed fully clothed. I should have had a hard time falling asleep, but instead the instant I closed my eyes I dreamed.

It started out harmlessly with the last stragglers from Rex's party sitting around looking bored. In fact, one of them even said so. "This town is Dullsville." There was general agreement and an added complaint about how hot it was.

Rex bounded to his feet, grinning, a general addressing his troops. "I have a plan," he announced. "Everyone pile into your cars and go get your swimsuits."

"Grantmere doesn't have a pool," Hayley pointed out.

"No, but it does have a reservoir." People weren't supposed to swim there, but his suggestion met with instant approval. The call for recruits was on. Ben was among those called up.

There were thirteen in all, and it was dark by the time they arrived. The heat of the day had cooled, and the wind made it pleasant to stand there. Finally someone ran forward and dived off the edge. He was poised in mid-air for an instant—I had time to recognize Ben's silhouette—before he cut cleanly downwards.

It was a beautiful dive, with his body straight and legs together. People whistled and clapped. Only I didn't. I stood there frozen, listening. Listening for the splash that never came.

The reservoir was empty.

I woke up gasping. With jerky, uncoordinated movements, I got up. What should I do?

There was only one thing I could do. I grabbed up the phone and dialled Ben's number. Busy signal. Anxiety clawed at me; no doubt it was Rex trying to talk Ben into coming "for a dip." The silhouette of Ben on the diving board was imprinted on my eyeballs. I hung up and tried again and again and again. The fifth time I even remembered to use the blocked cellphone.

On my sixth try the phone rang twice, and then a woman answered. Ben's mother? "Hello?"

"Hello. Could I speak to Ben, please?"

"Hang on, he's just going out the door." There was a slight clatter as the telephone was laid aside, and Mrs. Harper, yelled in the background. "Ben! Telephone."

I crossed all my fingers and even a few of my toes.

Pause.

"Hello?" Ben's voice held a tinge of impatience as if he could hardly wait to go out the door.

"Don't go out that door!" Fear vibrated in my voice, and I forgot to disguise it.

"What?"

I remembered to hold my nose and talk nasally. "Don't go out that door. You must not."

"Why? Who is this?" A note of wariness crept into Ben's voice.

I didn't answer, almost hung up, but first I needed to know that Ben would heed my warning.

"Who is this?" Ben repeated, louder. "What are you talking about?"

That spurred me back into speech. "Please, listen to me. Don't go with them to the reservoir. The dam's empty. If you dive in, you'll kill yourself. Please. They won't listen to me; you've got to phone them and warn them!"

Another silence. Then Ben said coldly, "How did you know about that? I didn't know myself until a few minutes ago."

I tensed. So it *had* been Rex on the phone.

"Who is this? I've half a mind to hang up right now," he threatened.

I babbled in an effort to keep him on the phone. "Don't hang up! You've got to listen to me!"

"Why should I?" Ben sounded angry. "I don't even know who you are."

"But I was right about the Science test, wasn't I? And I'm not lying now. Promise me you won't go anywhere near the reservoir tonight."

"No way," Ben said, shattering my hopes. "I'm not promising anything until you tell me who you are." I bit my lip, and his voice grew louder. "Tell me or I'm hanging up right now."

"No!" The word came out with explosive force.

"One last time. Who *are* you?"

"I'll do better than that," I bargained. "I'll come see you."

"Okay. You've got ten minutes, starting now." Ben's voice was likewise chilled. A click and the dial tone hummed in my ear.

I flew into action, running down to the living room where Suzy was. She had her textbooks spread all around her, but judging by the expression on her face she was doing more daydreaming than studying. She looked up guiltily. "I was just taking a breather—what's wrong?" She sat up, suddenly noticing my expression. "What is it?"

I cut her off. I had no time for questions. We lived ten minutes drive out of town. "I'm going out. And I'm taking the Green Machine. I should be back before Mom." I whirled out of the room.

Suzy followed me while I searched frantically for the car keys. Her blue eyes were wide with fright. "Where are you going?"

"Ben's," I replied without thinking and saw her mouth gape as I slammed into the Green Machine and roared off, driving as fast as I dared. I snuck a look at my watch. Eight minutes left.

I was a full minute late, screeching to a stop by the curb and jerking the keys out of the ignition. I was out and running by the time the engine shuddered to a halt. I slid to a stop in the grass when I saw a shadow detach itself from the steps in front of Ben's house.

"Hello?" Ben sounded uneasy, as if he were half expecting a ghost to pop out of the bushes. "I know you're out there, so you might as well come forward."

Light spilled out from the front porch of his house, and I took a few steps forward, still keeping my face in shadow. "Here I am," I said. My stomach knotted.

He peered at me. "Brianne?" Shock showed on his face. "Is that you?"

"Yes." I took another step forward.

Ben came down the steps to stand beside me. "What are you doing here?" It hadn't occurred to him I could be the caller, and a light bulb went off in my head. Maybe I wouldn't have to tell him after all.

I cleared my throat. "I got a phone call. Someone told me to come here right away or—" I gave a shudder that was not entirely feigned. "Or you would dive into the reservoir and die."

Ben whistled through his teeth and said simply, "Me too." His head was in shadow, and I couldn't read his expression. "I was just going out the door on my way to the reservoir when Mom called me back to answer the phone." He shook his head. "I'm telling you, Brianne, it's weird! The Science test and now this. I mean, why us?"

"I don't know," I said, feeling like the worst liar on the planet.

Ben sat back down on the cement front steps. "So I guess we wait."

I stayed standing, antsy. "Wait for what?"

"Wait for the caller to show up."

Oh, no. "What if he—she—whoever—doesn't? What if he just sent me instead?"

Ben's expression turned stubborn. "Then, in five more minutes, we drive to the reservoir and join the swim party."

"But—but—" The thought filled me with so much horror I started to stutter.

Ben squeezed my arm. "Don't worry, nobody's going to get hurt. The reservoir isn't empty."

"How do you know that? Have you been out there today?" I asked.

"No, but how could it be? And, even if it was empty, who would be stupid enough to dive in if there wasn't any water?"

"It's dark," I said. "Maybe they won't be able to see."

"It's still twilight, and there's moonlight. But it doesn't matter. The reservoir is not empty."

He was so certain, it made me angry, and yet he was right. How could the reservoir, thousands of litres of water, be gone? But I'd seen it in my dream, and my gut was certain that it would happen. "You're probably right," I told Ben. "But I couldn't live with myself if someone dove in and died and I could have stopped it. If we're going to go, let's go now."

Ben stood up. "We can take my pickup; the road to the reservoir is a little rough."

Ben snatched up a bag with a towel. I looked at it fearfully, and Ben said flatly, "There's water in the reservoir, and it'll look strange if I don't go swimming. I've got my swimming trunks on underneath so Mom wouldn't notice."

There were four other vehicles there when we arrived; their headlights illuminated everything but the reservoir. Two boys were having a towel fight while others cheered. I counted heads and was relieved to find everyone from my dream present and accounted for—no one had nerved themselves up enough to jump in yet.

Then Ben came out in his trunks, and my relief transmuted to fear. True to my dream Ben would be the first in.

He must have seen the stricken look on my face because he winked at me and picked up a small pebble, throwing it in before him. I heard a small *plop!* before Ben stepped up onto the makeshift diving board protruding from the dam wall. He walked quickly to the end of the board, bounced on his tiptoes and dove in.

It was a perfect dive—so like my dream that I felt a scream rising in my throat. My mouth opened, but at that moment I caught sight of Rex. His malicious expression shocked me into silence. I heard a splash.

I ran to the edge and peered over. Because of the dry spring the reservoir wasn't full to the brim, but there was water about two metres down. In the moonlight, I could make out black ripples as Ben swam towards the ladder.

"The water's freezing. Whose idea was this anyway?" He climbed out.

Someone tossed him his towel, and he dried off, joking with the other kids while I stood rooted to the spot. My legs felt weak, and I stared at Ben. When he dived in I had been so sure

—so very sure—that he would die. It seemed like a miracle that he was still alive.

In a minute Ben crossed over to where I was standing. "The water was a little on the cold side, but fine."

"Oh," I said, feeling stupid. "Good."

Ben just grinned. "I guess that's that then."

Instead of feeling relieved, I felt upset, as if I'd just discovered that two times two no longer equalled four. I desperately tried to reassess my dream. The first half had come true: Rex suggesting that the party move to the reservoir, Ben diving in. Just not the end.

Of course, now that I thought about it, the end of my first dream hadn't come true either. There hadn't been a spider diagram on my Science test.

"I'm sorry I kicked up such a fuss," I apologized to Ben. "I should have known better. It just seemed so real...."

"What?" Ben said.

Crap, what had I said? "I mean, the caller. What the caller described seemed so real." But my stammer and the horror on my face had given the game away.

Ben's eyes widened. "It was you. You were the one who phoned me."

chapter six

Time to stop lying. Time to change the surprise on Ben's face to disgust, if he was anything like my former friends in Edmonton. "Yes, it was me."

"But why?" Ben looked bewildered. "How?"

"It's complicated." I looked around. "I don't want to talk about it here."

My instinct for privacy was proven correct a moment later when Hayley came up to congratulate Ben on his dive and say hi. She was perfectly nice and friendly to me, but I didn't like the way she touched Ben's arm and said soulfully, "It's good to see you getting out more. We've missed you."

Ben treated her with distant politeness. "I'm always up for a swim. But Brianne has a curfew. I have to drive her home now," he lied. "See you Monday." He put a hand in the small of my back and steered me away from the crowd and over to the vehicles.

"Well?" he said when we were alone in his pickup. The determined expression on his face said he wasn't going to be stalled or fobbed off.

"Do you remember a news story last year about a hockey player's wife who was kidnapped and held for ransom?"

Ben looked wary at the seeming change of subject. "Conrad Tomlinsson's wife, yes."

"The night before she was abducted I had a dream," I said flatly. I'd told this story so many times to Dr. Geraldine that I didn't have to even think about it. Dr. Geraldine hadn't believed me and Ben wouldn't either, but I was damned if I was going to lie again. "In my dream, I saw a red-haired woman being grabbed as she hurried across a grocery store parking lot. I saw a man hold a knife to her throat. He taped up her mouth, handcuffed her, and threw her in the trunk of his car."

I stared out the darkened pickup window, not looking at Ben. I was vaguely grateful that he was listening, not scoffing and asking questions. "Then I woke up. I was scared, but I told myself that it was just a nightmare—until the next evening when I saw Philippa Tomlinsson's picture on the news. I recognized her.

"It wasn't the first time I'd had a dream that came true, but it was the first time it was about something important." Dr. Geraldine had always asked about those early dreams so I supplied a few details. "I dreamt that Aunt Elise went on a trip to Europe. That sort of thing."

I didn't tell Ben that I had enjoyed those small moments of prophecy, that I had thought the dreams were fun and wished I had them more than once or twice a year. How stupid I'd been.

"Anyhow, in my dream I'd seen the colour of the car she'd been kidnapped in and the first letter of the license plate, so I decided to tell the police what I knew. I mean, a woman's life was in danger."

I'd had enough caution to phone Aunt Elise first, spill out the whole story and ask her advice. She'd told me to go ahead and report what I'd seen, but to do it anonymously. "*The police won't believe you*," she'd said.

If I'd taken her advice and called the Crime Stoppers tips hotline, everything might have been okay. But I'd wanted to be involved, to know that I'd done good, so I'd lied to my dad and gotten him to take me to the police station.

"I knew the police wouldn't take me seriously if I told them I'd dreamed it, so I made up a story about hearing sounds coming from somebody's trunk while I was at a crosswalk, but the light changing before I could do anything about it."

It had been a stupid story, and the first thing Detective Reuter had asked me was why I hadn't gone to the police immediately. I'd told another lie and said that I thought I must have imagined it until I saw the news story. He'd thanked me, but I'd known from his face that he thought it was a false trail.

Until the tip paid off.

"The car turned out to be a rental, and they found it abandoned the next day. It had been rented under a false name, and the clerk hadn't been able to give a description of the man so the police had no leads. Detective Reuter came to see me and urged me to call him right away if I remembered anything more.

"That night I had another dream about Philippa. She was chained up in an unfinished basement. The lighting wasn't very good, but I saw the kidnapper a little better this time. Enough to know that he was big and had shaggy dark hair."

I'd seen Philippa more clearly. She'd been hugging herself the moment before, but the moment he came down the stairs she'd stood up and showed no fear. She'd yelled at him, telling him he was stupid and calling him bad names. I'd been terrified he would hit her, but all he did was take away her food and water until she 'minded her manners.'

"I phoned Detective Reuter and told him that I'd remembered that the driver of the car had been wearing a dark blue cap and his long hair had shown underneath. I told him that the driver's head had almost brushed the ceiling and he'd been so tall. He thanked me, but the details weren't much help.

"For the next four nights I kept dreaming about Philippa and her kidnapper. So I kept 'remembering' more details. I'd seen a bag of pet food in the back seat, because the kidnapper had a gerbil. I'd seen the kidnapper's eyes in the rearview mirror. They'd been brown and he'd had heavy brows. His nose looked like it had been broken. So many details, but none of them were enough to catch him." Remembered frustration crept into my voice.

I swallowed. "And then one night I dreamed that the ransom drop went wrong and the kidnapper decided to cut his losses and just kill her." *The kidnapper taking out his gun and brave Philippa throwing dirt in his eyes and locking herself in the bathroom. Philippa hiding in the tub while the door splintered under a hail of bullets and kicks.*

"I phoned up the police, nearly hysterical, and told them that he was going to kill her; that they had to hurry. Only I still didn't know where he was holding her." I stopped.

"They caught him, didn't they?" Ben asked hesitantly. "A neighbour reported gunshots and the police got there in time.

I remember that Philippa was reported as being in the hospital, but I don't remember what happened after that. Did she live?"

"Yes," I said. That at least had gone right. "She lived, the kidnapper was put in jail, and everything should have been perfect, but the next day Detective Reuter came to my school and arrested me."

The sheer humiliation of it crawled over me again. When I'd seen Detective Reuter I'd smiled. I'd had the stupid idea that he'd come to the school to thank me or even give me a medal. Instead he'd arrested me. He'd done it in front of my friends, and he'd chosen to do it there on purpose.

"What?" Ben said. "Why?"

"I'd told too many lies," I said. "They caught up with me. It turned out Detective Reuter had suspected me for some time, since the second or third dream. He had recordings of our conversations. He played them back to me, and it was quite damning. In the first recording he'd ask me if I'd seen anything in the back of the car, and I'd swear that it had been empty. Then in later recordings I would claim to have seen various items back there, clues that I'd actually seen in subsequent dreams. It was awful."

I snorted. "I broke, of course. I confessed that I'd never seen the rental car or heard Philippa pounding to get out of the trunk. I told them about the dreams. I talk for an hour straight, and when I'd finished Detective Reuter said, 'That's crap. You're going to learn something today, Brianne, and I suggest you learn it well: the police are not stupid.' And then he asked me how I'd met James Kidder, and he got mad when I said I didn't know who that was. 'The kidnapper,' he said, 'your accomplice.' The police thought I'd been in league with him all along, that I'd been taunting them by giving them little details, that I could have led them to Philippa and rescued her the very first day."

"My God," Ben said with feeling.

"Well, I learned something that day, after all," I said. "I learned that most people would rather believe that I am a horrible, horrible person than that I have dreams that come true." I looked at Ben, my lips trembling. "They confiscated my computer," I confessed. "They examined all the stories I'd written to see if I'd recorded any other crimes that James Kidder had committed. They read every scrap of my email in case I'd met him online and we'd carried out some sick cyber relationship."

"They were idiots," Ben said. He hugged me, folding my head against his shoulder. It felt very nice to be held. His acceptance was balm on a raw wound.

"You know," Ben said, "I kind of figured something had happened to you sometime. I thought it was your aunt's death. I never expected...this."

"What made you think something had happened to me?" I asked.

"There's a sadness in your eyes," Ben said.

It occurred to me that I'd noticed the same sadness in Ben's eyes.

Unfortunately, some other teens left the party just then and whistled at the sight of us embracing, spoiling the moment. I all but leapt back and Ben put the pickup in gear, bumping out of the field where everyone had parked.

Ben concentrated on the highway, white lines curving off into the darkness, and within minutes we were back in Grantmere in front of his house.

"Can you come in for a bit?" Ben asked. "I haven't heard the whole story yet."

I really didn't want to, but putting it off wouldn't make the rest of the story easier to tell, so I nodded.

Mrs. Harper met us in the hall. She looked at me curiously. "Hello." She had short, curly brown hair, and she was very thin. Too thin. Her wrists looked like sticks emerging from her pumpkin-coloured silk shirt.

Ben introduced us, and it was my turn to weather the parental barrage. I told her my parents' names, my dad's occupation and the fact that we were living in Aunt Elise's old house.

"We're going to go downstairs and listen to music," Ben told her. He took a step into the hall.

"Why don't you get out some pop and chips?" Mrs. Harper suggested. "Or would you prefer iced tea, Brianne?"

"Iced tea would be great," I said.

"Go make her some iced tea, Ben."

I started to protest that pop would be fine, but I caught Mrs. Harper's eye just then and realized that she was sending Ben away deliberately. She wanted a word with me.

From the resigned look on Ben's face, he realized it too. "I'll be right back." He went into the kitchen.

"I'm very pleased to meet you," Mrs. Harper said, her voice soft. "Ben's spoken of you. He says you were close to your aunt?"

I nodded, mystified.

"That's good. The two of you can talk to each other then. I'm afraid," Mrs. Harper blinked, and I realized that she was near tears, "that I've let Ben down because I can't talk about... well, you know."

I hadn't the faintest idea. I'd been starting to wonder if Hayley had broken Ben's heart, but that wasn't something that should make his mother cry.

"Be his friend, Brianne," Mrs. Harper urged. And then Ben came back with two glasses of iced tea and a bag of potato chips, and she said no more, only smiled tremulously.

The basement had garish orange carpet and older furniture, obviously hand-me-downs from upstairs, but a large screen TV and a huge sound system. Ben put on a CD, but he wasn't interested in the music, eyes trained on my face. "So what happened next, after you were arrested?"

I shrugged, trying to be casual, though I could still taste how terrified I'd been. "My parents got me a lawyer." I remembered how furious Dad had been at him for advising me to plead guilty, and implying I had colluded in the kidnapping, even though he himself had always had trouble believing in my dreams. Mom had simply got up and marched out of his office. The second lawyer was better. "I was lucky; James Kidder denied ever meeting me." I still got the shudders when I imagined what might have happened if James Kidder had decided to try to save himself by lying and saying that he did know me, that I was the instigator, that the kidnapping had been my idea.

As a result I'd been tried in juvenile court, not the adult one, and I hadn't gone to jail. In retrospect I'd been incredibly lucky, but at the time the psychiatric counselling the judge had insisted on had seemed like a slap in the face. He'd believed me to be guilty.

"And have you had lots of these psychic-type dreams?" Ben asked.

I shook my head. "Wednesday was the first time I had a true dream since the trial." I had had one other one in between my arrest and the trial, but reporting it would have only made me look more guilty so I'd kept quiet.

"You dreamed about the surprise test?" Ben asked.

I nodded confirmation.

"So what's the percentage?" Ben asked. "How often are the dreams right? Half the time? Twenty-five percent of the time?"

My face stiffened. "*All* the time."

Ben smiled, but he looked uncertain. "But that can't be. You were wrong tonight, remember?"

The reservoir hadn't been empty; Ben's life hadn't been in danger, but I shook my head stubbornly. It had felt true; it still felt true. Absolute and irrevocable. "Sometimes the dreams have symbols and I misinterpret them, but the dreams themselves are true."

Ben tried a different tack. "How do you know an ordinary dream from a true dream? What's the difference between them?"

"It's hard to explain in words." I paused, thinking. "I usually just wake up knowing I've had a true dream. It's like the difference between watching a movie on a movie screen and watching an IMAX film. It's deeper, clearer."

Ben looked skeptical. "How do you know it's not just your subconscious? Maybe you saw the tests in Mr. Darning's office, but had no conscious memory of doing so until you had the dream."

"I know because I had the dream before I went to Mr. Darning's office," I said.

"So maybe you saw them on his desk," Ben said. "What about tonight's dream? Maybe you fell asleep after Rex invited you to the reservoir and just naturally dreamed about that."

"Rex didn't invite me," I said.

Ben frowned. "He told me he did. Otherwise I would have phoned you. Are you sure he didn't call you?"

"I'm sure," I said tightly. Ben's doubt hurt. What did he think, that I was having memory lapses? I stood up. "It's late. I should go."

Ben walked me to the door and took my hand when I would have left. He looked thoughtful. "You really thought I was going to die, didn't you?"

I nodded miserably.

"Well, thanks for the concern. I appreciate it." He leaned forward and kissed me on the lips.

I didn't kiss him back.

Ben held my hand a little longer. "Are you mad at me?"

"A little," I admitted. I wasn't so much mad as tired of not being believed. Why had I even tried to tell Ben my side of the story?

"I'm sorry," Ben said, blue eyes sincere. "It's just...dreams that come true are a little hard to believe, you know. I promise

I don't think you're a horrible, horrible person." He tried to coax a smile from me.

It didn't work. "Yeah," I said, "you just think I'm crazy. What an improvement."

chapter seven

That night I dreamed about the other half of the story I had told Ben. I recognized the dream and tried desperately to wake up, but it was too late for that. A year too late.

It was early morning in Edmonton, very early and nobody else in the world was up but me. I'd just had a nightmare, and I was horribly, horribly frightened. Aunt Elise was going to die.

I'd seen her so clearly, at her computer printing out the prologue to a new novel. There was a crack of thunder, and the power went out. No more computer, and if she hadn't saved the file, no more prologue. The candles came out then and a pen. Aunt Elise furiously scribbled, ran out of ink and grabbed a pencil only to have the lead snap.

She heard a noise and went out into the hall. A gloved hand fired a gun, and Aunt Elise fell, a bloody hole in her temple.

I sat bolt-upright in bed, a screamed locked in my throat.

My first thought was to warn her. I rushed downstairs to the phone, but my fingers were shaking so badly I misdialled and had to hang up again. The phone rang under my fingers.

I snatched it up on the first ring and started to slam it down without listening. I didn't have time for conversation:

I needed that line! It didn't occur to me that people rarely phone for conversation at three in the morning.

"Brianne?"

"Aunt Elise?" I squeaked. "Is that you?"

"Yes." Her voice was calm. "It's me."

"Thank God." I gulped in air. Words poured out of me like water escaping from a dam. "I've just had the most awful nightmare. In it you—"

"Died. I know." Aunt Elise's quiet words shocked me into silence. Her voice became heavy with regrets. "Oh, Brianne, I'm sorry you had to be involved in this, but maybe this way you won't make the same mistakes I did."

My fear heightened. What was she talking about? She sounded as if she were really going to die! I realized that I had wanted reassurance. "What do you mean? Now that I've warned you, you can be careful—you don't have to die!"

"Yes, I do." Her voice was sad but calm. "But first there are some things I must tell you. About your dreams—"

"Who cares about my dreams?" I practically screamed into the receiver. "Aunt Elise, you've got to protect yourself! Lock all your doors, do something! Don't die!" Tears ran down my cheeks.

Then she said a strange thing. "It's too late; I've dreamed my own death. Brianne," and now there was urgency in her voice, "listen to me. There are things you should know."

"I know you're going to die!" I burst out. What could be more important than that?

"Be quiet!" Aunt Elise overrode me. "We don't have time for this. The wulfdraigles are watching—"

I opened my mouth to ask what the wulfdraigles were, but just then I heard the crack of a gunshot. "Aunt Elise?" I called. "Aunt Elise?" I jiggled the phone, but she did not answer. I redialled, but the line was dead. And so was she.

I'd woken Mom and Dad, frantic. Mom had repeated the call I'd tried to make, but, of course, she couldn't get through either. "You probably heard thunder, Brianne. The telephone line went down, that's all." Despite her words, Mom had looked worried.

"No. You're wrong. He shot her. He shot her in the head."

Mom flinched, then made up her mind. "Okay, here's what we're going to do. I'll call Elise's neighbour and ask them to check on her. But, Brianne, not one word about what you saw in your dream. We only mention what you actually heard on the phone—and we say that I was the one who phoned her, not you."

Dad looked uncertain, but Mom overruled him. "If Elise is...hurt, there will be an investigation. Questions. I will not risk Brianne being implicated in another crime."

Mom had made the phone call, apologized for the late hour, but expressed her concern. Then we'd waited, me, in tears, Mom, wrapped in a layer of cold ice that hadn't cracked until we'd found out it was true: Aunt Elise was dead.

The police called it suicide, and Mom hadn't let me suggest anything different, but I remembered the gloved hand with the gun, and I knew she'd been murdered.

I woke up shivering, so cold I was almost stiff. I sat in my bed for a few moments, trying to block the dream images out of my head. When that didn't work, I swung my feet over the edge of the bed and padded, barefoot, down to the kitchen. My throat felt parched and dry.

Lissa met me there. Her eyes were very wide, and moonlight touched her sleep-tousled brown hair.

"Lissa!" I whispered, stooping down to her level. "What are you doing up?"

"Waiting for you," she whispered back.

I straightened. "Waiting for me?" I struggled to keep the tremor out of my voice. Sometimes Lissa frightened me. Because if I dreamed true what did she do? In a very real way she was one of my dreams come true. The first one.

When I was seven years old and angry with Suzy for scribbling in my colouring book, I had had a dream about having a different sister. A nicer sister with hair the same colour as mine. I'd liked the dream and wished it came true. Nine months later Lissa was born.

From the very first there had been something a little otherworldly about Lissa. As if she drifted through this world like a ghost without being truly connected to it.

And she knew things that she shouldn't.

"I had a bad dream, too. There was a fire." Lissa looked up at me, expression troubled. "Will it rain soon?"

"I hope so." I kept my voice light. "Thanks for keeping me company, but I'm all right now. So you just trot on back to bed, okay?"

"Okay." She went back to her room and crawled back under the covers. While I was tucking her in she asked, "Brianne, what's a fall girl?"

"You mean a fall guy," I corrected, smoothing down her bedspread.

"No, I mean a fall girl." Her brown eyes were so wide and serious I couldn't help but smile as I explained.

"It's someone who ends up getting blamed for the crime while the real bad guy gets off scot free."

"Okay." Lissa watched me leave with unblinking eyes.

I felt better then, more normal, and continued to the kitchen. I poured myself a glass of chocolate milk and sat down, tucking one leg under me while I drank it.

I had just drained the last drop when the phone rang. The skin prickled on the back of my neck. The clock read three AM—the same time Aunt Elise had phoned me.

I picked up the receiver. "Hello?"

"Hello, Brianne," a male voice said. "The wulfdraigles are still watching you."

I slammed the phone down, totally unnerved. My hands shook, and my mind shrieked questions. I felt hunted, trapped. I didn't want to be, but I was still there when the phone rang again. I snatched it up before it could rouse Mom. At this time of night she would assume that a single ring was a wrong number. I held the phone between my thumb and one finger delicately as if it were a snake. This time I just listened.

"Did you think we had forgotten about you, Brianne? Your aunt protected you for a lot of years, but she's dead." The voice turned soft with menace. "You've had a year's grace, more than most of us get, but that year is up now."

A sudden suspicion filled my mind, and I interrupted. "What do you mean 'protected me'? I don't know what you're talking about."

There was a small pause and then a soft laugh. "Oh, but I think you do. I think you know as well as I do." A sulky note crept over the line, and I was sure.

"Hello Rex," I said, my fear replaced by anger. "What are you doing up so early?"

"Well, well, Brianne," Rex mocked, making no effort to disguise his voice. "How very clever of you."

Rage licked through me. How dare he phone me up in the middle of the night and scare me half to death? "YOU—YOU—" I could think of no word strong enough.

"Conduit," Rex supplied, amused.

"Conduit? A conduit for what?"

"For dreams. They pass from the world of dreams through us into our world. The wulfdraigles find us very helpful."

My anger died, leaving me very cold. "I'm not a conduit—whatever you called me. I'm not helping the wulfdraigles."

"Oh yes, that's right," Rex said with false cheer. "You're still just a true dreamer, but you'll take the next step and become a conduit soon. The wulfdraigles have ways of dealing with true dreamers who don't swear to serve them." I heard a threat in his words before he continued smoothly, "You and I have a lot in common, Brianne."

"I doubt it. My DNA isn't half reptile," I shot back.

Rex ignored the insult. "You're not the only person in the world to have dreams. Once you've asked the wulfdraigles to make your dreams came true—the real dreams you have when you're asleep, not some silly daydream—they've got you. And you asked them, didn't you? Out loud?"

"No!" It wasn't quite a lie. I hadn't asked the wulfdraigles because I hadn't known they existed, but I *had* wanted my dream about Lissa to come true. Had I said the words aloud? I couldn't remember for sure, but I suspected I had.

Rex overrode my denial. "You gave the wulfdraigles permission to make your dreams come true. You opened a passageway between the real world and dreams, and no matter how hard you try to plug it up, it's going to stay open. For good. Or should I say for worse?"

I was silent, appalled.

"Did you really think they'd go away and never come back just because you willed them to?" His voice changed, became bitter. "Dream on, Brianne. *Dream on!* They'll always be there—until you die."

"No," I said, but my fear showed in my voice.

"You almost died in Science class. The spider was about to poison you. If I hadn't touched the back of your neck and woken you at the right moment, you'd be brain-dead in a coma."

Now I was supposed to believe that Rex was some kind of hero, who'd saved me? Riiiight. "If you're their servant, why would you want to stop them?"

"Yeah, the wulfdraigles were pretty pissed at me the next time I dreamed," Rex admitted. "I got treated to the whole voice-of-thunder routine. You owe me for that. I managed to convince them that you weren't stupid, that you'd realize how hopeless opposing them is and join us instead."

"Never," I swore.

"You'll change your mind." Utter confidence.

"Who are you?" I demanded, my voice low and intense.

"Who am I? Or who *was* I?" Rex sounded almost desolate. "I used to be normal. Now I'm Rex, your friendly neighbourhood conduit." His voice hardened. "The wulfdraigles can make your dreams come true, Brianne. Or your nightmares. The choice is yours." There was a loud click as the connection was cut.

I sat there, receiver still in hand as I had so many nights ago when Aunt Elise had died. Nobody was dead this time, but I felt the same cold, gripping fear I had then. What was I going to do?

I paced. I was on my fifth circuit around the living room when the big orange dictionary caught my eye. The memory of Lissa paging through it looking for "wolf draigles" returned.

I collapsed into a sitting position on the floor and pulled the thick tome onto my lap. I flipped through the pages with an abundance of nervous energy.

Nothing remotely related under wolf or wulf. No entry under draigle at all. Nothing relevant under conduit. Nil, nada, nothing.

I was about to close the dictionary when a folded down corner a few pages forward of wolf caught my eye. Had Lissa found something I'd missed?

I skimmed down the first column: wallaby, wallet, wall-eyed, wallflower, wallop, wallow, wallpaper, Wall Street, walnut.... A pencil mark caught my eye. Walpurgisnacht, which was German for Walpurgis Night.

There were two meanings given, both of which made my blood run cold. One, an event or situation having a nightmarish quality. Two, the Eve of May Day on which witches ride.

I slammed the dictionary shut. Aunt Elise had died on April 30. Walpurgisnacht.

chapter eight

I stumbled through most of Sunday in a daze. I answered the telephone once in the afternoon and heard Rex say, "Hello," for one awful moment before Suzy's voice came over the extension obviously delighted, "Rex!" I put the phone down as if burned. I'd forgotten about that small problem.

The phone rang again an hour later. I didn't think much of it until Mom poked her head out of the living room. "Brianne? Your dad's on the phone. It's your turn to talk to him."

I'd meant to tell Dad that Suzy's new boyfriend was bad news, but Dad's first words knocked the thought right out of my head. "Your mother tells me you've been asking about the wulfdraigles."

The way he said it so matter-of-factly made me jump. Not "something about wolves" but "the wulfdraigles."

"Yes," I tried to keep my voice steady even though my pulse was thudding. "I remember Aunt Elise mentioning them, and I wondered what they were. Mom said she didn't know." There was a hint of a question in my voice.

Dad sighed. "Yes, she told me that, too. I'm afraid your mother associates the term with a rather bad part of her life, something she doesn't like to talk about."

"Then you know what they are?" I asked, betraying my eagerness. I had to find out. "Where do they come from? What do they look like?"

"Oh, but they don't exist." Dad sounded surprised. "I thought you knew that. They were just something your Aunt Elise invented. They were kind of her muse. She called them her inspiration."

Inspiration. My stomach did a slow roll. Aunt Elise had written horror novels, and the wulfdraigles had inspired her.

Dad was still speaking, and I snapped my attention back to him. "I know you've always looked up to your aunt—and she was an admirable woman—very intelligent—but she had her fair share of peculiarities. The wulfdraigles were just one of them. For a while your mother was afraid she was going to crack. Those horror things she wrote didn't help."

"Was she crazy?" I asked, barely daring to whisper.

"Oh, no!" Dad said. "Just a little eccentric, as a lot of people who live on their own seem to get. Not that she was a recluse, she was always throwing some kind of party." Dad lapsed into his own remembrance.

"Did I ever tell you she was the one who introduced your mother and me? I'd crashed this party—I found out later it was to celebrate her first bestseller—and I tried to pick her up." Dad sounded amused. "She gave me this funny look and said I had the wrong sister. She led me over to where your mother was sitting, introduced me as your mother's future husband, and then left.

I was pretty miffed at first—it was damn awkward. Then your mother apologized, we started talking, and that was it.

The rest is history." He paused. "I've always wondered what made her so sure I belonged with her sister."

I clutched the phone, small waves of panic rising in me. I thought I knew. Or could guess. I suspected Aunt Elise's dreams had come true too.

I wondered if Mom had known. If Aunt Elise had embarrassed her the way I sometimes embarrassed Suzy.

Dad changed the subject, and I followed along. I asked about the fire, as usual, and Dad tried to play it down but the cold front had brought high winds. The fire was definitely out of control and had eaten up close to 2,900 hectares. Dad was calling from Douglas Hills because the town was being evacuated.

"Keep safe," I told him and passed the phone to Suzy.

I went over what he'd told me about the wulfdraigles. A few of my questions had been answered but not many. The big ones remained. Aunt Elise had known, but she was dead now. I wished I'd kept my mouth shut and listened to everything she'd been trying to tell me the night she'd died. If only she had left some kind of message....

That was it! I sat suddenly upright. The prologue Aunt Elise had been so desperate to get down on paper even after her computer stopped working. She had left me a message. Maybe.

But where to find it? We had sold some of Aunt Elise's possessions at a garage sale, but I felt sure Mom would never have thrown out Aunt Elise's writing.

I was reluctant to ask Mom, so, on the basis that she knew everything, I asked Lissa. I was not disappointed.

She led me straight to a box in the corner of the basement. I lugged it out into the middle of the rumpus room floor and sat cross-legged in front of it. Lissa sat beside me, brown eyes avid.

I opened it, removing the contents one by one. Three postcards fell out of a map of Germany, and I picked them up curiously. Aunt Elise had gone on a trip to Europe just before her death, and I hadn't received a souvenir from her.

All three postcards were in rough shape, bent and mangled. The pictures on the front all showed hills. I flipped one over to read the description, but that was so smudged only one word remained: Brocken.

To my surprise the postcards were addressed to Brianne and Lissa Foster. Our old Edmonton address was printed in the top corner, but they had never been mailed. I squinted at Aunt Elise's spiky handwriting in one corner. "They were defeated here once," I read and stared without seeing ahead of me. They who? Could she have meant the wulfdraigles?

The other two postcards contained no message, and with a kind of half-shiver half-shrug I laid them aside. I found what I was looking for at the very bottom of the box.

PROLOGUE — 1,000,000 years ago

Burn and flicker. Flicker and burn. Man-thing watching the flames feels eyes grow tired, struggle to close. Man-thing rubs hairy back of hand across bad eyes. Stares into fire. Does not look to the side. To the side is darkness. Fearful cold darkness. Not good to look at. Watch fire instead even if it makes eyes tired. Flicker. Burn. Flicker. Flicker.

There is movement off to side in heart of darkness, but man-thing sees it not. Man-thing watching flames. Pretty orange flames dancing against black background.

(Black. Dark. No. Won't look there. Watch pretty flames instead.)

Tired eyes see picture there. Rub eyes again, but picture does not leave. Man-thing peers closer, hypnotized. Sees wavery line and picture-dream beyond. Man-thing has been honoured by Dream God. Watch pictures. Watch man-self-thing become great honoured chief of tribe.

Flames sputter and go…

From here on the words continued in pen. The power must have gone off then—just as the flames died a million years ago. It was an eerie coincidence, and I didn't like it. Not one little bit.

…out. Great honoured chief does nothing. Great honoured chief is not afraid of darkness. Easier to dream in darkness. Darkness is not to be feared. There is nothing to fear—

Teeth sink deep in neck of man-thing. Blood spurts.

Screams. Howls. Trapped in the darkness, man-things run. Are hunted.

Man-things form circle of spears with young ones in the middle. Smell of fear. Noises in the dark. Scrape, scrape. Wulfdraigles drag away their prey to eat.

Dawn pushes back dark. Plains empty again. Only numbers have changed. Less man-things. Work resumes. Pick up tools. Bundle babies and food.

Here the pen changed to pencil, smeary and hard to read.

One boy stands alone. Hates. Mother, sister, brother. All dead. Mother, sister, brother. Hands clench. Power grip. Swears hatred on wulfdraigles. Swears by his blood that all wulfdraigles, everywhere, will die so that man-things will be forever safe.

Two skipped lines, then some jotted notes at the bottom:

—Boy succeeds in exterminating the wulfdraigles, BUT unbeknownst to him some of the wulfdraigles take refuge across the dreamline (perhaps killed while sleeping? magic ritual?)

—wulfdraigles trapped in a world made only of dreams for millennia, sending nightmares to terrorize humans. Pain and fear are meat and bread to them. They enjoy our terror, but more than anything what they want is to escape their prison, to return to our world and make it run red with blood.

—Chapter one, present day, begin with a wulfdraigle crossing the dreamline and preying on a young woman.

A squiggly line. No more messages. Aunt Elise must have phoned right afterward.

I reread the prologue and the notes twice to see if I had missed any more clues. If there were clues. What if Dad was right, and the wulfdraigles were just a figment of Aunt Elise's imagination? Since they were the topic of a book she'd been writing the night she died it might explain why she had mentioned them to me on the phone. But not Rex. The simple explanation part of me wanted to believe so desperately would not explain Rex and his uncanny knowledge.

Which left the other explanation: that the wulfdraigles were real, not fictional, and Rex spoke to them in his dreams; that thousands of years ago the skeleton I'd seen at Rex's house had been a live animal related to wolves that preyed on humans; that the wulfdraigles had power over dreams; that my dreams weren't a psychic talent I'd been born with, but an evil gift from creatures who fed on pain and fear.

There were some large puzzle pieces still missing, but at least now I had some idea who the wulfdraigles were. I could name my enemy. But what did they want to recruit me for? Why did they send the black widow spider to kill me?

If I was important enough to kill, then did I have some power? A way to hurt the wulfdraigles?

"C'mon," Lissa said, making me jerk in surprise. I had forgotten she was even there, she had been so quiet. I waited with bated breath for her to say something spooky. Something that showed she knew what was going on with my dreams and the wulfdraigles.

"Come on," Lissa repeated, "Walt Disney's starting."

Or maybe not.

I gave a short crack of laughter and followed her. I waited all the rest of that day for something to happen, but it didn't, and I fell into bed exhausted. I felt as if I'd run a marathon: my eyes just would not stay open a minute past ten.

For a change I slept like the dead. Suzy was the sleepy one the next morning.

"What time did you go to bed?" Mom asked, after Suzy's third smothered yawn.

"Eleven." Suzy stopped to yawn again. "It took me awhile to fall asleep, and then I woke up at two in the morning, outside. I must have been sleepwalking."

"Outside?" Mom asked in surprise. Suzy had had occasional bouts of sleepwalking since she was a child. They'd decreased as she'd grown up, but weren't uncommon. What was unusual was Suzy leaving the house while sleepwalking. I couldn't remember her ever doing that before.

"I might be half way to South America by now," Suzy joked, "but I cut my foot on the gravel and woke up."

I didn't crack a smile. Suzy's sleepwalking disturbed me. Couldn't anyone sleep through the night anymore?

Monday proceeded in a mockery of normalcy. I was hyper-aware of Rex. Every time he entered the room I would tense up, waiting for him to drop some new and hideous surprise on me. I had a hard time concentrating on my surroundings. Even on Ben.

"—want to eat outside today?" Ben asked at noon.

I tore my gaze off Rex and forced a smile. "Sure." I told myself that I was lucky my tale of woe and nightmares hadn't driven Ben off.

Why then, did I feel so resentful?

Once we'd found a spot out on the football field, Ben smiled at me. "So, had anymore dreams lately? You didn't dream I fell off a cliff or got struck by lightning or anything?" he continued.

He was just teasing me. I knew that. But to me it wasn't remotely humourous. "Don't make fun of me," I said sharply.

Ben stopped smiling. "I'm not, Brianne, I promise. But I just can't take psychic powers seriously."

I didn't have psychic powers. According to Rex, the dreams were sent to me by the wulfdraigles, but Ben didn't believe me so there was no point in talking about that. Even so, I was mad. "Why can't you take them seriously?" I demanded. "You know, there have been plenty of people besides me who saw visions throughout history. Cassandra, Nostradamus. How do you know they're not real?"

Ben's face flushed with temper and something else. "I know because of Chris!" He was genuinely upset.

I blinked. "Who?"

Ben stared at me.

My own anger started to drain away. "Ben? What's wrong?" I touched his arm. His muscles were corded with tension.

He swore. "Shit. I'm sorry, Brianne. I thought you knew."

Knew what?

"Everyone else knows...." He turned away and spoke to the football posts. "Chris was my brother. He died last year. He was my twin."

"Oh, no." For a moment I was paralyzed, then I remembered how I'd felt when I lost Aunt Elise. I hugged Ben from behind. "I'm so sorry."

His body stayed tense, a stone statue, but I kept hugging him, and he moved jerkily, covering my hand with his own, pressing it to his heart. He seemed incapable of speech.

It would have been cowardly to change the subject, and I had a sudden flash of insight: Ben wanted to talk. If he hadn't, he could have just changed the subject. I spoke around the lump in my own throat. "You said you were twins. Were you identical?"

Ben nodded.

"How did it happen? Was he...Chris...sick?"

Ben shook his head. I thought he wasn't going to be able to say anything, but after a moment he rasped out an answer. "He was hit by a car. Hit and run."

My heart broke for Ben. His twin hadn't been murdered like Aunt Elise, but there had been the same lack of justice in both cases. It became clear to me why Ben was such a careful driver.

"He was killed instantly," Ben said.

I didn't know what to say. It was good that Chris hadn't lingered in pain, but I knew how much had been left unsaid between Aunt Elise and me, how much I regretted not saying in our brief conversation. How much worse it would have been for Ben. I rubbed his back.

"You know how...in movies...the other twin always knows that something has happened?" Ben asked. "Through some special sense?"

I nodded. He couldn't see me, he was still facing away, but he went on.

"Well, I didn't. I didn't have a clue. I was at home when the phone rang. Mom answered it, and I saw her face go white. She said Chris had been hit by a car. I drove her to the hospital, and the whole way I swore to her that it was going to be okay. That Chris was my twin and that I would know if he were hurt really bad, but I didn't. He was dead when we got there. He was dead the moment the car hit him."

For the first time I understood why Ben wouldn't—couldn't—believe in my true dreams.

I scrambled forward in the grass on my hands and knees so that Ben couldn't avoid looking at me any longer. I put my hands on his shoulders. "It's not your fault," I told him. "The fact that you didn't feel a psychic bond with him doesn't mean you didn't love him enough, or that his death didn't rip you apart. You loved him."

Ben was crying. "Yeah, I did. He was my twin."

I tried to think how I would feel if I'd lost Suzy or Lissa, only losing a twin would be even worse. "You were best friends as well as brothers," I said.

"Yes. Even though Patrick would tell you *he* and Chris were best friends. It's funny, once we started high school, we didn't hang out together as much at school, but we would look at each other sometimes and I would know exactly what Chris was thinking and vice versa. Exactly. And at home, it was just like always. Two peas in a pod." His voice cracked. "Mom used to call us that."

My throat ached. I wanted to say, 'I'm so sorry, Ben,' but he would have heard that a lot already. If he felt the way I did after Aunt Elise's death, right now he needed me to listen more than he needed sympathy. "Tell me what he was like," I said.

"He was like me," Ben said, his expression bleak. "Mostly. But he liked baseball better than basketball. He never could do a decent lay-up. He always put way too much ketchup on his hotdogs and hated mustard. He was more social than I was."

"He was a party dude?" I guessed, remembering what Patrick had once called Ben.

"Yes. He loved parties. He dated more than I did. He was such a flirt." Ben laughed ruefully. "It used to make his girlfriend mad, so Chris would tell her I'd been the one flirting not him, and she'd punch his shoulder for lying."

A dim light bulb went off in my head. "Did he go out with Hayley?"

"Yes."

I felt a small surge of relief. Hayley had been Chris's girlfriend, not Ben's.

"Hayley was always breaking up with him and getting back together the next weekend. She liked the drama of it. Chris didn't seem to mind." Ben's tone said he didn't understand why he hadn't minded.

"I can't believe no one told you," Ben said, making eye contact. "I swear I wasn't keeping it from you, Brianne."

I nodded to show that I believed him.

"I just assumed someone would have mentioned it. But maybe I shouldn't be surprised." Ben looked bitter. "Nobody talks about Chris any more. At least not in front of me. I think they're afraid I'll break down and cry, or something."

I gently wiped away a tear that had run down Ben's cheek. "You can cry in front of me. You can talk about Chris, and I'll talk about Aunt Elise and we'll have a regular Kleenex bash."

But Ben wasn't ready for jokes yet. "I hate them for it," he confessed. "I want to shout at them: he existed! He mattered!"

"You miss him," I said. "But just because your friends no longer talk about Chris doesn't mean they no longer think about him. They're just uncomfortable. Patrick must miss your brother too. That's why he invited you to his party."

"Patrick thinks I am Chris, or just like him, anyway." Ben clenched his fists. "He wants me to become his best friend and take Chris's place. But I can't do it."

"Of course, you can't," I said staunchly. "You're you."

"You say that because you never knew Chris," Ben said.

"No, I didn't know him," I said. "I wish I had." I had a sudden thought. Was that why Ben liked me, because I was the one person who would never compare him to his twin?

I decided I didn't care.

"Chris died, and I became his ghost," Ben said painfully. "Just looking at me reminds Mom that Chris is dead. She turns away, so I won't see her cry. The sight of me hurts her. I've started always clearing my throat or making some noise before I go into a room."

"What about your dad?" I asked. I didn't even know if Ben's parents were still together or if they'd divorced years ago.

"Dad spends hours in the basement, tying flies. We used to go fishing together, the three of us. Dad talks about going again this summer, but I know we won't. It would hurt too much." Ben stared up at the sky. "The house is so quiet," he whispered.

"Your mother told me she wants to talk to you about Chris," I said. "She thinks she's failed you by not being able to talk about it."

"Poor Mom. She's started to see a therapist, but I don't think she talks to him either. I think she spends her whole time in his office painting red and black abstracts." Ben smiled briefly. "They're starting to fill up the house."

"What about Hayley?" I asked. "Can't you talk to her about Chris?"

"Oh, *her*," Ben said. "I did for a while. She really was devastated when Chris died, but then she began to get into the whole grieving thing. She started wearing black all the time and putting on this air of tragedy." He made a face. "She went out with Rex three weeks later. She said it wasn't a date, but it was."

Rex again.

"Was Rex friends with Chris?" I asked cautiously.

"Yes," Ben said. "They were a bit more friendly than Rex and I are, but they weren't especially close. Why?"

"No reason." I gave a brief, meaningless smile. "I just wondered."

Ben looked like he wasn't sure if he believed me or not. I never was a good liar.

chapter nine

Suzy wasn't on the bus that afternoon, and when Lissa and I got off I saw Rex's car parked aslant in our driveway, blocking both Mom's car and the Green Machine.

In the living room, I found Rex was sitting on the sofa, between Mom and Suzy, looking at photo albums. "Hey, who's the cowgirl?" Rex asked. "Is that you again, Suze? Snazzy boots." He winked at her.

My mother was charmed. Her face told me that quite clearly. She had been nice to Ben, but not like this. She laughed at every punch line.

Then there was Suzy. My throat closed up just looking at her. Beyond a shadow of a doubt I knew why she had skipped school and disobeyed Mom to go to the movies with Rex. She was infatuated; her eyes didn't once leave Rex's face.

Lissa came and stood by me, putting her cold hand in mine. "Suzy says he's an angel," she whispered. "But he's not. I don't like him." She hurried off to her bedroom as if she was afraid, and a wave of protectiveness swept over me.

I stepped into the circle. "Hi, Rex."

"Hey, Brianne." Rex revealed no surprise over my entrance. "You sure used to have a lot more hair." He tapped the photo album. "Why did you cut it?"

"It was time for a change," I lied.

Mom got up and excused herself, regretfully. "I have to get started on supper. Rex, you're welcome to stay. We're having spaghetti and meatballs."

"I'd love to," Rex said warmly. If I hadn't known he was a snake, I would have fallen for it, too.

"Are you sure?" I asked. "It's homemade, not catered like your party."

Suzy frowned—as I'd guessed the party was still a sore point for her. Unfortunately, she got over it quickly, smiling with dazzling intensity at Rex when he said he liked homemade better. He returned the smile, volt for volt. I might have been a fly on the ceiling for all the notice they took of me.

I tried to restart the conversation and pull his attention away from Suzy. "It was a great idea of yours to go swimming in the reservoir."

"If it was, why did you leave early?" Rex asked.

Suzy snapped out of her trance long enough to echo, "Yes, why did you leave, Brianne?" She stressed the word *leave*, a hint that she didn't want me around right now.

The phone rang, sparing me from having to answer. Seconds later, Mom called from the kitchen. "Suzy, it's for you."

Suzy looked annoyed, but sprang up. She breathed, "I'll be right back," in Rex's direction and hurried away.

Which left Rex and me alone.

I got straight to the point. "What are you doing here?"

Rex bared his teeth. "Isn't it obvious? I'm here to see your sister."

"Lay off," I said, clenching my hands into fists. "You're not welcome here."

Still he smiled. "Suzy invited me." Then, with an abrupt change of topic, he said, "You know, I think I rather like talking to you, Brianne. There's no need for pretense between us. You know who I am, and I know what you're going to be."

"And what's that?"

"A conduit, just like your aunt was."

I was on my feet without being conscious of how I'd gotten there. "That's a lie." Aunt Elise had been the nicest aunt in the world; she would never have helped the wulfdraigles.

"Well, I do lie a lot." Rex shrugged. "But this time I happen to be telling the truth. Think about it. The wulfdraigles feed on human fear, and your aunt gave people nightmares for a living. She helped the wulfdraigles for years."

I pounced on his phrasing. "What about last year? Was she helping them then?"

Rex smiled. "Your point. She dug her heels in and refused to cooperate. Which is why they killed her."

Aunt Elise had been murdered. I'd always known it, but it still shocked me to hear it said so bluntly.

"Take warning," Rex said. "Don't let it happen to you. The wulfdraigles will make you an offer soon. Make sure when they do you accept. Your dream tonight will be a test to prove your worthiness to become a conduit. Stop trying to warn people about what you see in your dreams. And don't try to get between Suzy and me either. The wulfdraigles are watching you. If you tell, there will be a penalty."

My heart was beating too fast, but I lifted my chin. The wulfdraigles scared the crap out of me, but Rex was as human as I was. "Oh, yeah, like what?"

Rex's eyes were as hard as flint. "I'll tell the whole school that you were arrested last year. I bet you wouldn't like Ben to know. I'll tell him first."

Ben already knew. The thought gave me courage. "Go ahead," I said. "It's not a secret. It's bound to come out sometime anyhow."

I'd surprised him. Rex leaned forward, studying me. "It wouldn't bother you to become a freak and an outcast again?"

I folded my arms. "I lived through it once. I can do it again."

"And what about Suzy?" Rex's eyes flashed. "She'll get trashed along with you. She'll lose her friends all over again."

In that second I truly hated him for trying to manipulate me by using my love for my sister. "You creep. I wish she could hear you now."

"You're not paying attention. The wulfdraigles tried to kill you last week. I stopped them. If you don't get with the program soon, a little gossip is going to be the least of your worries. They. Will. Kill. You."

I remembered Philippa. My life would have been a lot easier if I'd never told the police about my dreams, but she might be dead—without my warning the police might not have responded to her neighbours 911 call so quickly. "The wulfdraigles are evil. How can you help them? How can you live with yourself?" Loathing filled my voice.

"There are rewards," Rex said, after glancing away. "The money, the car. A great face and hot babes like your sister."

I felt ill. "No doubt," I said, striking back with all the force I could muster. "If it weren't for your expensive car and your looks, Suzy would never go out with you."

I had just enough time to see I had scored a hit—Rex paled—before Suzy burst out with a horrified, "Brianne!" from the doorway. Then to Rex, "She's wrong!"

Rex got up with pretended stiffness and said, "It's all right, Suzy. If you don't mind, I'll take a rain check on supper and go home now." He left, head down, like someone who had just been stabbed in the back.

"How could you say such a terrible thing?" Suzy rounded on me. "I like Rex for a lot of reasons and none of them have to do with his money."

Behind Suzy's back, I could see Rex eavesdropping while he put on his shoes. "You seemed pretty excited about his fancy car."

Suzy put her hands on her hips and glared at me. "I was excited that he *trusted* me enough to let me drive his sports car. He didn't flinch when I opened it up to 130 on the highway, and when I told him I'd love to race on the NASCAR circuit he said I should go for it, that I had the guts."

Flattery, I wanted to say, but Suzy wasn't finished yet.

"I have *fun* with him," Suzy said. "He almost makes up for having to live in this crappy town—which I had to move to because of *you*, I might add."

I bit my lip, struck hard by guilt. Before I could rally, we both heard the front door close.

Suzy's eyes lit up. She hadn't realized Rex was still there. She whirled and ran after him as if her life depended on it.

I watched through the living room window as Rex stopped at the last possible moment, allowing her to climb into the sports car beside him. She talked a blue streak, but didn't manage to convince him to stay for supper. Finally, she kissed him—for way too long—and got out again. He roared off.

Then Suzy came back inside. I met her on the porch. "There are things you don't know about Rex."

Suzy made a scoffing noise. By unspoken agreement we went down the hall to our room where we could fight without Mom overhearing.

I owed her an apology. "I'm sorry for what I said. I had no right to imply that your feelings for Rex were superficial." I'd just hoped.

"No, you didn't. So why did you say it?"

I took a deep breath. "He goaded me into it."

"How?" Suzy asked. "By being nice to you?"

"No. Rex is a different person when you're not around." I paused. The last time I'd mentioned the wulfdraigles to Suzy, she'd blown it off. If I told her the rest of it, she would think I was crazy. I settled on something she would understand. "He knows about my being arrested in Edmonton. He threatened to tell the whole school."

"What?"

"He knows about my arrest," I repeated.

Suzy's eyes filled with stars. "He knows and he still wants to go out with me? How long has he known? When did you tell him?"

I felt like shaking her. "I didn't tell him. That's the whole point. He threatened me, Suzy."

She shook her head. "You must be wrong. Rex wouldn't do that to me."

To her? "He can and he would," I said flatly.

"No," Suzy said stubbornly. "He wouldn't. Trust me, I know Rex better than you do. If he said something like that, it was because he lost his temper. What did you say to him just before? Were you arguing?"

"Yes," I admitted. We'd been arguing over whether or not Aunt Elise had been a conduit.

"There you go, then," Suzy said.

I found her stubbornness maddening. I tried to remain calm. "There's a good reason why I don't trust Rex—"

Suzy held up a hand. "Wait a second. If you didn't tell Rex about being arrested, who did?"

"I think he might have dreamed it."

Suzy's expression turned skeptical. "Highly doubtful. I bet it was Tillie. She has a crush on Rex, and she's been mad at me ever since he asked me out. Damn, she could have told half the school by now."

"It wasn't Tillie," I said. The wulfdraigles had told Rex, but I couldn't just blurt that out. Suzy would think I was crazy. "Look, it doesn't matter how he found out, okay? The point is, Rex knows."

Suzy stared at me as if I'd suddenly grown purple antennae. "Of course it matters who told him. We need to come up with a strategy, a way of countering the story if it comes out. We need damage control."

"No." I shook my head, feeling a hundred years old. "The story's going to come out sooner or later. There's nothing we can do but ride it out."

"Ride it out?" Suzy looked at me in disbelief. "I feel like I don't know you anymore. The arrest changed you. You're so serious now. You hardly ever laugh."

Her accusation stung me. I still laughed—didn't I?

"But at the same time," Suzy continued, "you're so much stronger now. You can ignore the gossip, but I can't. I care what they say about us. I'm not proud of it, but I do."

"It's—it's not that I don't care," I stammered. "Of course, I do. But," I struggled to explain, "I know inside that I didn't do anything wrong. I still have my...my honor, as hokey as that sounds, and that protects me, at least a little."

Suzy didn't get it.

I changed the subject. "About Rex, don't you think he's just a little too good-looking, a little too perfect?"

"Oh, my God." Suzy put a hand to her throat. "Rex was right. I didn't believe him, but it's true. You're jealous! That's what this is about."

I blinked, unable to believe my ears. Me? Jealous of Suzy over Rex? It was so far from the truth as to be almost ludicrous. "You've got it all wrong—" I started.

Suzy cut me off, looking at me with a mixture of contempt and pity. "Don't lie, Brianne. Rex told me about the way you keep following him around and phoning him up. You even invited yourself to his party."

My own temper rose. "That's not true. I went to the party with Ben, and let me tell you I like him better than I'll ever like Rex!"

Suzy caught the distaste in my voice and turned red. "Is that so?" she retorted. "You have a funny way of showing it. If I were you, I'd pay more attention to Ben if you want to keep him."

Wonderful. Just what I needed. Dating advice from Little Sister—who was seeing somebody that made Dracula look good. "He's dangerous," I told her. I had to find some way to get through to her. "Just look at the snow job he's done on you. You've only been going out with him for a week. How can you take his word over mine?"

For a moment, I thought I had her. Suzy looked stricken, but then Mom called us to supper, and the moment was lost. Her expression closed, and she stopped talking.

After supper, as usual, Mom turned on the television to watch for news of the Douglas Hills fire. It was hopeful. The wind had shifted enough so that it seemed likely that the town would be saved, though the evacuation order had stayed in effect. "With one hundred and ninety-two smaller fires also burning in the province resources are stretched thin," the reporter finished.

The weather report called for scattered showers and nothing more.

That night I dreamt of lightning. Black clouds rolled in, blotting out the light of the moon and stars and replacing it with flashes of lightning. Bolts of enormous power and voltage split the sky in half.

Lightning struck a tree, knocking it over, and small sparks leapt between it and the ground. In a minute the forest litter of twigs and leaves was ablaze. The clouds moved away without giving so much as a drop of rain. Meanwhile, the ground fire climbed the ladder of a half-fallen tree and reached the treetops. A faster moving crown fire started.

Hands on my shoulders grabbed me, pulling me from my dream. "Brianne, wake up! You have to wake up!" I opened my eyes and saw Lissa bending over me, face pale and eyes huge with fear.

I sat up. "What is it?"

"It's Suzy," Lissa gasped, already tugging me up from the bed. "She's sleepwalking."

I ran down the hall after Lissa. The front door flapped open, and through it I saw the white smudge of Suzy's nightgown disappearing into the garage. I started to run.

Sharp rocks stung my feet, and I remembered that that was how Suzy had woken up last time. Why was she still sleeping?

No time. I whipped around the corner into the garage, and grabbed Suzy's arm as she was about to climb into the Green Machine. From past episodes I knew Suzy could often be steered back to bed, without even waking up. "No, Suzy," I said. "Let's go back in the house. You don't want to go driving in your nightgown, do you?"

She didn't fight me, but she didn't hear me either. She just kept pulling, trying to get into the car. Like a zombie. Her eyes were focussed straight ahead, her face slack.

"No, Suzy, let's go this way." I tried to turn her shoulders away from the car.

Stubbornly, she kept trying to go back to the car. My feet were freezing; I couldn't believe Suzy hadn't woken up yet. Finally, in desperation, I pinched her arm, hard enough to bruise it. "Wake up!"

Suzy blinked and rubbed her arm. "Ouch! What'd you do that for?"

I sighed in relief. She was awake. "You were sleepwalking. I couldn't wake you up."

Suzy's face changed. "I wonder why that was," she snarled, stalking out of the garage.

"What?" I trailed after her.

Suzy didn't answer, speeding up.

I ran after her, wincing as the gravel cut my feet. How could Suzy bear to walk so fast? Didn't her feet hurt? Then I saw why they didn't.

She was wearing shoes.

The first time she'd sleepwalked the sharp gravel had woken her, so this time she'd stopped to put on her shoes first.

The hairs on the back of my neck rose. I paused, and then hurried after Suzy. I caught up with her in our bedroom, tearing the blanket off her bed. "Suzy, what's wrong?"

"It's your fault I've started sleepwalking again." Suzy flung the words at me. "Remember? Stress makes them more likely." She snatched up her pillow and quilt. "I'm going to sleep in the living room. Maybe I'll be able to get some rest there."

Rex was to blame, not me. I knew that, but I still felt hurt.

"Don't worry," Lissa said, startling me. I'd forgotten she was there. "I'll wake you up if she sleepwalks again."

I stared at my slightly spooky sister and believed her. Something inside me relaxed, letting me go back to bed, though it was a long time before I got back to sleep.

I resembled the walking dead the next morning. Suzy must have already given Mom some sort of explanation about the change in sleeping arrangements because she didn't say anything, only watched me with worried eyes.

I bided my time until Mom and I were alone in the kitchen. "Mom?" She looked up at me from her pancakes, mouth full. I tried to sound casual. "If Dad calls, could you tell him to watch out for popups this morning? I thought I heard some thunder last night." Popups were small fires that, if not controlled, could grow into large fires and make a second firefighting front.

Mom swallowed and studied me. "There was no storm last night. But I'm sure that if the Forest Protection Branch's automatic sensors detected any lightning strikes, they'll send out an aerial patrol to look for any new fires. You know that."

I also knew that a fire could grow from a single lightning-struck tree to fifty hectares in fifteen minutes. I forced a smile. "I guess I'm just a little worried about Dad, that's all."

Mom laid down her fork. "You've had another dream, haven't you?" It was more a statement than a question, but I blushed. So much for casual.

She went on. "And in the dream I suppose there was a lightning storm and a forest fire?"

I hesitated for a split second, remembering Rex's warning not tell anyone about my dreams. But Dad needed to know, and I didn't really believe the wulfdraigles could be watching me every minute. I mean, they lived in dreams and I was awake. So I nodded. "Yes. I dreamed it."

Mom remained calm. "Under the circumstances, it sounds like you've had a very natural, very run-of-the-mill nightmare. Frightening, yes, but, Brianne, everyone has them. I have them. Your father has them. Suzy has them."

"Lissa has them."

She smiled. "No doubt Lissa does."

"No, Mom." I was in over my head now. "Lissa had the dream about the fire, too. She dreamed it on Saturday."

This time annoyance did show on Mom's face. "A coincidence, Brianne, that's all. Lissa's been listening to the same talk about the fire that you have."

I was almost certain Lissa's dreams, like mine, came true. Although I suspected her power was greater than mine. Or would be once she grew up. But that was besides the point. I tried to keep my voice even when what I really wanted to do was scream at Mom to listen. "I know the difference between a true dream and a regular dream."

Mom looked stubborn. "It was just a dream."

"If you don't believe me, does that mean you think I lied about the kidnapping dreams, like the police do?" The thought devastated me. Mom's rock-solid belief in me had helped me through some very bad days. Had she changed her mind? Had she never believed me at all?

Mom winced. "No, Brianne, no. Of course not."

"Then why won't you believe me now?" I almost wailed.

Mom just looked at me. "You remind me more of her every day," she said at last.

I struggled to understand. "You mean Aunt Elise?"

"Yes. She was my sister and I loved her. But sometimes I didn't like her very much. She was so bloody...enigmatic and sure that she was right and no one else. I wish you weren't so much like her." She studied the bottom of her coffee cup. "It scares me."

It scared me, too, especially given Aunt Elise's current mailing address.

"I lost Elise to the dreams," Mom said. "I won't lose you too. You have to stop having them, Brianne." Her eyes bored into mine.

I stared. Did she think I wanted to dream, that it was some bid for attention? "I can't just will them to stop." I tried to explain. "The wulfdraigles send the dreams, not me."

Mom made a frustrated sound. "And now you're starting Elise's stupid obsession with her so-called wulfdraigles, blaming everything on some make-believe creatures! Just stop it! Make up your mind to stop dreaming now, Brianne. I don't want to hear another word about them and that's final!" The coffee cup was set down with a bang.

I blinked back tears. "So I should just ignore the fact that we're in danger?"

Mom looked militant. "Yes, that's exactly what I want you to do. If you ignore the dreams, they'll go away."

Right. Just ignore them. That would be a lot of help.

"Well, Brianne?" Mom asked coldly.

My face felt stiff, but I gave her the answer she wanted. "I won't bother you with my dreams again."

When I was arrested, it was the worst thing that had ever happened to me. I'd gotten through it because my family had stood with me. Dad had had his doubts about my dreams, but Suzy and Mom had believed in them and in me. Now neither of them was listening to me, and Lissa was too young to be much help. I was truly on my own.

chapter ten

The instant I got on the school bus I knew that Rex had carried out his threat. Everybody stopped talking and stared at me. They knew that I'd been arrested for aiding and abetting a kidnapper. The seat where I usually sat was taken.

Apparently the wulfdraigles had been watching me, after all.

"You should be in jail," Hayley's brother said.

I felt myself turn into stone. Despite what I'd said to Rex, I'd been hoping this day would never come.

"Hurry up and sit down," the bus driver said.

Rather than go where I wasn't welcome, I sat with Lissa in one of the few remaining empty seats, directly behind the driver. If making me sit with the little kids was supposed to humiliate me, they didn't know me very well. After what I'd endured in Edmonton, this was nothing.

"Suzy, come sit with me," Hayley called.

Her brother glared at her, and she rolled her eyes. "It's not Suzy's fault her sister's a nutcase."

Suzy stopped halfway down the aisle. "My sister is *not* a nutcase. Who told you she was?"

Suzy's unexpected loyalty brought a lump to my throat. Whatever Rex had done, we were still sisters.

Hayley looked offended at having her magnanimity thrown back in her face.

"Sit down!" the bus driver yelled.

Suzy didn't budge. "Not until she tells me who's been telling lies about my sister."

"I bet I can guess," I said under my breath.

Suzy heard me and I received a scorching glare of my own. "*It wasn't him*," she mouthed. "Spill, Hayley."

Hayley tossed her head. "Tillie told me, but it's *true*. I saw the picture."

I knew what picture she meant. Because of my age, I hadn't been identified by name in the newspaper photo, but they'd caught my face full on. I flushed and had to remind myself forcibly that I hadn't done anything wrong.

"Sit down, now!"

Suzy sat down next to me. "I told you it wasn't him."

I couldn't keep silent. "We don't know who told Tillie." Rex had used Tillie as his mouthpiece before.

"Shut up."

I didn't argue, but instead bent my head toward Lissa. "Lissa, some people may say bad things about me today. You can tell them that they're wrong, but don't get into any fights, okay?"

"Okay." Lissa's face was more solemn and serious than any eight-year-old's should be, and made my heart twist. Damn Rex.

The rest of the morning was just as rotten.

Nobody sat by me in home room. Nobody smiled or said hi. Some boys blew spitballs in my hair. My elbow got jostled in the hallway. I dropped my books, and when I bent pick them up, a boy stepped on my hand.

I got called names under people's breath. Criminal was about the nicest. I thought blackly that I hadn't known how good I'd had it when they only called me Miss Muffet.

The only person who wanted me to talk to him was a creepy boy who asked me if I'd gotten a share of the ransom. I glared at him and walked away.

As I'd expected from last time, the hockey fans were the worst. The boy who had his locker next to mine wouldn't let me open it. He didn't move until the bell rang, so I was late for Science.

Mr. Darning blasted me when I came through the door, and I stood there blank-faced through his lecture. Did the teachers know, too? Could I expect slews of detentions like at my old school?

Ben, I noticed, had saved a seat for me. The gesture brought me nearer to tears than any of the hassling and name-calling I'd endured so far. He looked worried, but motioned me over.

If I sat by him, he would become a pariah too.

If anybody deserved to be an outcast, it was Rex. While Mr. Darning's back was turned, I yanked Rex's stool out from under him and sat down. I kept my eyes on the front as Rex murmured something to one of his friends and everyone moved down a space.

I avoided Ben at lunch too, and after that he seemed to take the hint. I told myself it was for the best.

By the time school let out I was ready to tackle lions. Instead, I cornered Rex in the hallway.

I started simply, my voice deceptively calm, “Did you make Suzy sleepwalk?”

I had the satisfaction of seeing Rex jerk, and for a moment his eyes showed a flash of some emotion not unlike—fear? No, that couldn’t be right. Swift control hardened Rex’s features, and he ignored my question. “Have pleasant dreams, Brianne? They come true today.”

My turn to flinch, as I suddenly saw roaring flames. For a brief second I was back inside my nightmare. “No!” I shook my head to clear it.

“Oh, yes.” Rex’s eyes were blank and empty. I followed his gaze and gasped when I saw my dream there in the hallway. Only a thin, wavering line separated it from me. The rest of the kids could not see it; they walked right through it, disappearing and then reappearing on the other side.

“What is *that*?” I asked, taking a step back. “Are you doing that?”

The dream and the line followed me, staying in front of me wherever I turned.

Rex seemed amused by my ignorance. “That’s the dream-line, the divider between our world and the world of dreams.”

“Why can’t anyone else see it?”

“The wulfdraigles rule the world of dreams. Most people have a built-in rejection of them, and rarely remember their dreams. Only a very few have rich dreams, memorable dreams, that the wulfdraigles can shape and mold. Those are the people they target, people like you and me. The wulfdraigles send nice dreams to trick us into wishing our dreams came true," Rex explained. "Making the wish creates a link between the wulfdraigles and the true dreamer. Every time you dream afterwards, the line between our world and theirs grows thinner. The dreams the wulfdraigles have shaped leak out—come true. That's the only way the wulfdraigles can influence our world. Most true dreamers can't handle it. They go insane—unless they take the next step."

A wave of cold terror passed over me. For one horrible moment I saw nebulous forms in the flames. Maniacal wolfish faces full of fury and hatred.

From Rex's expression, he saw them, too.

"What do they want?" I asked.

"What does every mass murderer rotting in his jail cell want? Freedom, so they can rip and rend and tear. Since they can't cross the dreamline, they have to settle for a different kind of sustenance. They feed on fear and pain. That fire you've been dreaming of? That's the wulfdraigles' idea of a feast. Death on a platter."

"We can't let them do it!" I burst out. The picture Rex was painting was too horrible. "There has to be some way to stop them."

"We?" Rex turned cold, dead eyes on me. "You forget who you're talking to. I'm not just a true dreamer anymore, I'm a conduit." He turned, boxing me into a corner. "We let the wulfdraigles send us what dreams they want and keep our mouths shut. That's the smart way. It's true dreamers like you who resist that are rare."

I refused to shrink back against the wall. "I won't let you do it." I glared at him.

"How do you plan to stop me?" Rex was unconcerned. "Will you warn everyone? I don't think they'll listen to you." He jerked his chin to indicate the unfriendly attention we were receiving. "You can't stop the fire, Brianne. Be reasonable. Save what you can."

Give in, he meant. Become a conduit. Stop warning people about the nightmares the wulfdraigles sent me. I closed my eyes, shook my head.

"Tell the wulfdraigles when you change your mind—when the fire reaches your house. Just don't leave it too late, or they may decide they're better off with you burned to a crisp. Bye, bye, Brianne." He strolled away.

I closed my eyes for a brief moment, trying to will some strength into my limbs. When I opened them again, I looked straight into the deep blue eyes of Benjamin Harper. He looked disgusted and pained at the same time. While I watched, he slung his backpack over his shoulder and headed out the door.

I wanted to run after him just like Suzy had after Rex, but I decided there was no point.

I had already missed the bus, so I walked aimlessly in what might or might not have been the direction of home. I didn't want to think about what Rex had just told me, but I couldn't stop myself. The wulfdraigles....

I was crossing the street when the dreamline reappeared, and I saw the dream world within it. I stopped dead, but it didn't matter.

Fire had reached Grantmere, and orange flames licked at my feet. Pavement doesn't burn, I told myself, but I could feel the soles of my shoes warming and jumped like a scalded cat.

Wind sent a blast of heat in my direction. The fire leapt higher, surrounding me, and deep in the flames I could glimpse the faces of the wulfdraigles. Bestial faces, long snouts, malevolent eyes...they were laughing. I could hear their unholy glee.

Screech! Even the noise of a pickup braking to a stop mere inches from me didn't pull me out of my dream. Someone swore, but it was only when a hand touched my shoulder that I startled awake.

I turned, heart thudding, and for a moment it seemed my worst fears had come true. Ben's face was superimposed over the faces in the flame so it looked as if they were one.

I almost screamed, but Ben shook me, dispelling the dream. "What's the matter with you? Don't you know any better than to stand in the middle of the street with your eyes closed?"

Ben didn't give me a chance to respond, grasping my arm roughly. "Come on. I'll drive you home. You might not make it on your own."

I followed him like a sleepwalker. In a way I was. The flames were still there, a fiery spot in the middle of the street, and I could not tear my fascinated gaze from them. I was only dimly aware of Ben's frown. I climbed into the pickup beside him and sat staring like a zombie.

The flames swam in my vision turning everything orange.

In desperation, I reached out and touched Ben on the elbow before he could move his pickup out of neutral. "Ben." With some difficulty I got his name out.

"Yes?" He turned an impatient gaze on me.

I could see the fire reflected in his eyes, and I shuddered. "Talk to me. Please. It doesn't matter—" I swallowed "—

about what. Just talk." Ben looked as if he was going to make a sarcastic remark, and my nails dug into his sleeve. "Please," I begged. Rex had said that some true dreamers went insane; I didn't want to be one of them.

The wildness in my eyes must have convinced Ben because he parked on the side of the road and talked to me.

"So what do you want to hear about? The weather? That one's real popular at my house. There are supposed to be wind gusts tomorrow. Crap, I hate talking about the weather. How about hockey? The Oilers are trading Conrad Tomlin—okay, maybe not such a good idea. C'mon, Brianne, you're freaking me out here," he complained.

Replying was beyond me. I pleaded with my eyes.

"Okay, okay." He sighed. "If all you need is for me to talk, why don't I practice my presentation for Ms. Scott's class? Prepare to be bored out of your skull. Coal-mining in Grantmere..."

I heard only random snippets of his speech, but that didn't matter. The sound of his voice mattered; it was my link to reality. "...discovered by town founder Robert Grant...the foothill north of town...The mine closed when Robert Grant was declared insane...."

After about fifteen minutes, when the fire had faded out, I stopped him. "Thanks, Ben. You can quit now, I'm back to normal."

His temper flared up. "Back to normal as compared to what? You nearly got yourself killed back there! What's wrong with you? You scream in the middle of Science class, you phone people up and tell them about your dreams, and you take a snooze in the middle of a street!"

"Yeah," I agreed, head down, sunk deep in misery. "I guess that about sums it up."

Ben swore. "Do you see that?" He pointed out the window, and I saw a coffin-shaped traffic sign that said Fatality. Someone had tied a bouquet to it. I had a terrible feeling that I'd seen those particular flowers in the Harper's garden.

Ben's next words confirmed my hunch. "That's where Chris was hit. Where he died. It's bad enough I have to drive by it every time I leave the school, now you...." Words failed him.

"Oh, Ben, I'm so sorry. I didn't know." I reached across the seat and took his hand. He let me hold it, but didn't squeeze back. "I know what you mean. The first month we moved into Aunt Elise's house I could hardly bear to go into the kitchen where they...found the body. I kept picturing her there dead and—you know." I made a face.

Ben nodded. "It was a closed casket, wasn't it? I remember the funeral director saying so when he was convincing my mom to do the same for Chris."

I was about to tell Ben I wouldn't know if it had been closed casket or not since my arrest had kept me in Edmonton, when my ears registered what I'd just heard. "When did Chris die?" I asked.

"A year and a month ago almost exactly," Ben said.

It was June 4th today. "What date?"

"May 1st."

The day after Aunt Elise. "Oh, my God," I said as my mind made another connection.

"What?" Ben asked. He scratched at the back of his wrist.

I was too rattled to lead up to it. "Your brother may have been murdered."

Ben's grip on my hand turned bone-crushing. "What did you say?"

I turned sick eyes on his face. "I've always believed that my aunt was murdered. Tell me, did Chris go out to see Hayley that night?"

Ben's face paled. "Yes."

"He must have seen the murderer leaving," I said. "Witnessed something. The murderer must have been afraid of being identified when news of Aunt Elise's death got out so he staged a hit and run accident."

"*No.*" Ben looked sick, furious. He pounded the steering wheel, honking the horn once. "*No.*"

I didn't say anything, watching him with pity and empathy. I knew he believed me.

"Who?" he asked.

I shook my head. "I don't know." Rex, I thought. Rex would have recognized Chris's car and known who was dating Hayley.

"Don't lie to me," Ben said, blue eyes intense.

"I *don't* know. I only have suspicions."

"Who do you suspect? What makes you think your aunt was murdered?"

I took a deep breath. "I know that she was involved with something bad," I said. "Just before she died, she started to write an exposé on it. That's why they killed her."

"They who?"

"I don't think I should tell you," I said. "I don't want to put you in danger."

"I have a right to know who killed my brother!"

"And if I tell you who I suspect, what will you do? Go to the police? They won't listen. Try to take matters into your own hands and maybe end up in jail?" I shook my head. "No." After last year, I didn't trust the police not to jump to conclusions.

"Your aunt was murdered," Ben struck back. "Are you just going to let them get away with it?"

His words hurt. "They've already gotten away with it. If I see a chance to put them in jail, then yes, I'll take it. But I don't see one right now."

Ben thumped the steering wheel again. "Damn it!"

"After what happened last year, a policeman wouldn't take my word for it if I said the sky was blue, much less started nattering about dreams."

"Why didn't you defend yourself today?" Ben asked. "Why didn't you tell everyone you were innocent?"

"Previous experience," I said bitterly. "If the friends I had for years didn't believe me, then there's no chance that people who've only known me for ten months will."

"I believe you. Why wouldn't you talk to me today?" Ben asked. He scratched at the back of his wrist again.

"I didn't want my bad reputation rubbing off on you."

Ben looked angry. "Yeah, right."

I got angry, too. "What do you mean by that? It's the truth."

"I'd have an easier time believing that if you hadn't spent all day cozying up to Rex. You sure didn't seem worried about his reputation."

Ben was jealous. It took a moment for the idea to sink in. I'd had so many things happen to me today—all of them bad—

and now this. It was mind-blowing. I laughed in sheer relief. Ben was jealous. Of Rex.

My laughter died as Ben angrily turned the key in the ignition. I tried to think up words to refute what Ben had said, but couldn't come up with any, so I reached across the seat, grabbed Ben by the ears and kissed him, plastering my mouth against his. "I like *you*, not Rex!"

He didn't look convinced so I kissed him again with all the conviction I could muster. He kissed me back, furiously, hands in my hair, but when he drew back he still looked unsure.

"If you don't like Rex, then what were you talking to him about?" Ben asked. "You always seem to be watching him."

My tongue stuck to the roof of my mouth. I could hardly say we were threatening each other. "I'm afraid of him," I blurted out.

"What?" My four-word sentence was obviously the last thing Ben had expected to hear.

"He scares me. He's dating my sister, Suzy, and I'm afraid of what might happen to her." No lies so far. "Remember our first date? Suzy was with him in his car. That's why I was so stunned to see him. She snuck out to be with him; Mom grounded her for skipping class that day."

"Okay." Ben nodded. "I can see that. If I had a sister, I wouldn't want her to date Rex, but that doesn't explain why you're afraid of him. Unless you think he's involved in your aunt's death."

Ben had guessed. There was no point in hiding the truth any further; Ben would just blunder in blind if I didn't tell him. Plus the temptation to confide in someone was too strong to resist. Maybe Ben would know what to do. If he believed me.

I started at the beginning. "The first time I noticed there was something wrong with Rex was when he lied and said I phoned him. I didn't."

"What?"

"I didn't tell him about the test. I freaked when he started talking about telephone calls in nasal voices."

Ben was silent for a minute, then he smiled. "Suzy must have overheard you and warned him herself."

I shook my head. "And Suzy thinks you must have called someone who called Rex. Never mind, there's other stuff too. The day of the party he told Tillie Gerard to repeat to me something Aunt Elise had said to me in my dream the night before. And after I got home from the reservoir he phoned me up and threatened me."

"Threatened you how?"

I told him how Rex had said I no longer had Aunt Elise's protection and that I would have more dreams come true. "He said he worked for something called the wulfdraigles. He called himself a conduit," I said.

I could see that Ben wanted to know what wulfdraigles were, so I told him about the skulls and the prologue my aunt had written without coming right out and saying that I believed in them, too.

"Then yesterday, Rex said he would tell everyone at school my secret if I didn't stop warning people about my dreams."

"Which he did," Ben said. His jaw set. "Warning people about what?"

"Yesterday and today I dreamed of fire. Forest fire. Grantmere's going to go up in smoke." I shuddered, the memory of the flames too fresh for calm discussion.

Ben rubbed his forehead as if he had a headache. "This is all a bit much to take."

"I know." I'd known, but I'd hoped otherwise. "So you don't believe me." A weight seemed to settle on my chest.

Ben hesitated. "I keep remembering the night Rex phoned me to invite me out to the reservoir. I asked him if I could invite you too, and he laughed. He said that you'd already received your own personal invitation, but there was something in his voice when he said it, like he knew a joke I didn't."

"Yeah, Rex would think my dream was funny," I said.

"I don't want to think about this anymore," Ben said. "I'm not feeling well." He touched his forehead again, and I noticed he was sweating.

"Are you okay?" I asked him as he restarted the motor.

"I'm not sure." Ben swallowed. "I feel a bit sick."

"Do you want me to drive?" I asked. I didn't have much experience with stick shifts, but I could probably drive Ben home.

I was alarmed when Ben moved over for me to take the steering wheel. I'd been expecting him to insist that he was well enough to drive.

That anxiety was nothing to what I felt a moment later when I signalled to pull out and saw a spider web attached to the rear view mirror with a glossy black spider hanging upside down in it, red hourglass markings showing clearly on its abdomen.

A black widow spider.

chapter eleven

Oh, God. This was why Ben felt sick; he'd been bitten. My first dream was coming true. I moaned.

"What is it?" Ben asked.

"See that?" I pointed. "That's a black widow spider."

Ben squinted at it. His eyelids looked swollen. "Aren't black widows poisonous?"

"Yes, but they seldom kill," I said. "There are only a couple of spider deaths a year and usually only if the victim is very old or very young or—" Or very allergic. I didn't finish my sentence. "When were you bitten?"

Ben shook his head. "I don't know. Maybe I've just got the flu."

"Your wrist," I remembered. "You scratched at it a couple of times." I reached over and grabbed it. There, among a fine dusting of black hairs, I found it. A small red bump, slightly warmer than the rest of Ben's skin. "I've got to get you to the hospital."

In my panic, I tried to treat the pickup like an automatic and shift straight into Drive. It didn't work. The knobbed stick shift wouldn't move. I swore and tried again, remembering to use the clutch this time.

The engine stalled as I lurched a foot out of the parking space.

Ben didn't say anything, eyes closed, which scared me half to death. Sweat poured off of him.

I took a deep breath, focussed, and restarted the engine. This time I made it out of the parking spot and onto the road. When the speedometer hit 25 km/h, I clutched again and managed to shift up into second gear. The pickup felt a lot higher above the road than driving a car.

We got to a corner, and I signalled left, toward the hospital. Turning required shifting back down into first and then up again. This street was busier, which made me sweat.

Unless sweating was a symptom and I'd been bitten, too.

"Stop!" Ben yelled.

I slammed on the brakes in the middle of the street. The sudden jarring movement knocked the spider from her web. She fell. I lifted both feet off the floor, but that made the pickup roll forward so I put my left foot back on the brake. I brushed frantically at my jeans in case it had fallen there. "Did you see where it landed?" I asked Ben.

Ben didn't answer. He flung open the door and vomited. He leaned so far over I was afraid he might fall. I lunged and grabbed his shirt, pulling him back. "Are you okay?"

"No." Ben groaned, doubled over. "My back hurts. Cramping...."

I wanted badly to get out of the pickup, but Ben looked bad. "Hang on," I told him. "We're almost at the hospital." I put my right foot down and clutched back into first gear. We rolled into motion—and I nearly hit a white car that had gotten impatient behind me and decided to pass.

Grantmere wasn't a very big town, and the hospital was only six blocks away, but the drive seemed to take forever. I kept twitching, imagining that I felt spider legs walking over my skin, imagining that I felt bites. It was an effort to keep my eyes on the road, to keep from searching the pickup for the spider.

I parked, badly, in front of the hospital and started to take off my seat belt. Then I saw the spider, crawling across the seat toward Ben.

I didn't want to hit it with my hand and risk getting bitten myself. "Ben! Get out!"

He fumbled with his seat belt while I looked around for something to hit the spider with.

Step on a spider and it will rain. I wrenched off my running shoe and tried to hit it. I missed, and it scuttled faster. At least this one didn't triple in size, I thought, raising my shoe for another blow.

"No," Ben said hoarsely. He'd gotten out of the pickup and was clinging to the door. "The doctor may need to see it. Don't squish it."

I could see the sense in that—black widows weren't native to Alberta and the doctor might not believe us without proof—but I had no handy container to trap it in so I hastily got out of the pickup and shut the door. In one sock-foot and one shoe, I went around the hood of the pickup and helped Ben close his door. "Here, lean on me," I said. I helped him walk into the hospital and gratefully turned him over to the nursing staff.

I stayed nearby while we waited for the doctor and helped Ben answer their questions. Then the doctor finally arrived. He seemed happy enough to take my word for the spider's species—I could have killed it after all. He gave Ben a painkiller and some antivenin and told Ben he would be just fine. "But we're going to keep you here for observation for about eight hours, okay?"

"Don't call my mom," was all Ben said. "Let me call my dad; he'll pick her up."

I understood what Ben meant. His mother would be terrified to learn that another son was in the hospital.

Fifteen minutes later, Ben's parents rushed in. Neither of them spared me so much as a glance, and I faded off into the background. From the lobby, I called home myself, explained to Mom that I was late because Ben had taken sick, and asked her to pick me up at the hospital.

I remembered the spider while I was waiting, but a trip out to Ben's pickup found it locked up tight—with the keys inside. Oops. Back inside. I snagged Ben's dad, explained about the keys and the need for the spider to be killed before anyone drove the vehicle again, and had to leave it at that.

Suzy picked me up in the Green Machine. As soon as I got inside, I saw that her eyes were red-rimmed. She'd been crying; my stomach lurched in sympathy. Her day had probably been almost as bad as mine had.

"I'm sorry you missed the bus," Suzy said, after I'd told her that Ben was going to be okay. "I told the bus driver to wait, but that witch Hayley told him that you'd told her you weren't coming." Suzy's anger showed in her driving. She put her foot down before we were out of the town limits.

"It's okay," I said. "I'm glad I was there to help Ben."

"You were right." Suzy turned stricken, remorse-filled eyes on me. "It was Rex who told about what happened in

Edmonton. I tracked down Tillie and asked her who'd given her the story."

"And what did Rex say?" I asked after a pause.

Suzy flipped her blonde hair back, outrage crackling in her blue eyes. "He said that you'd annoyed him, and he'd had to teach you a lesson, but that he didn't hold your criminal past against me. He said he was still *willing* to take me to the prom—as if he was doing me some huge favour."

I was astonished. I'd been sure Rex would come up with some story shifting the blame onto someone else. He could have said that Tillie lied, for instance. He had to have known what Suzy's reaction would be to his condescension.

"He said that you should cooperate next time. What did he mean?" Suzy demanded. She slammed on the brakes as if punishing Rex and barely let the turn light blink once before roaring onto the gravel road that led to our acreage.

I was too tired to explain it all again—and I couldn't forget that Suzy hadn't believed me about the wulfdraigles last time. "Rex knows about my dreams," I said, boiling things down to the essence. "He wants me to stop trying to prevent some of my dreams from coming true."

"How long has he known about your dreams?" Suzy asked.

"Since at least the day that I screamed in Science. Probably before," I said as she parked in front of our house.

Suzy wasn't stupid. She figured it out. "It's not a coincidence that he's been dating me, is it?"

"No. He's been using you as a threat to hold over my head," I admitted. Suzy needed to know, but I didn't like hurting her.

Suzy's eyes showed pain, closely followed by hatred. Suzy never did anything by halves. "He's going to regret that," she said, more to herself than me.

If Mom had asked Suzy how her day had been, I think Suzy would have told her everything, but when we walked in the door we found Mom kneading bread. Suzy and I had a private sliding scale for judging how worried Mom was about Dad's work. Dusting was mild anxiety, scrubbing floors was bad. Kneading bread, when we owned a bread machine, meant that Mom had run out of regular chores to do.

While Suzy kept Lissa distracted with a game of Monopoly, I quietly turned on the TV. I soon found out that the Douglas Hills fire had grown to 3,200 hectares and was now cutting east, bringing it closer to Grantmere. Worse, there was a report that several firefighters had been taken to the hospital with burns. It was almost certainly not Dad—someone would have called us—but Mom still worried and so she made bread.

I had inherited that from her, the inability to keep still when I was worried. I prowled around the house that evening, staring out my bedroom window at the faint rose colour of the sky in the east which was due to fire and not sunset.

As I watched the band of red enlarged itself. Oh, God, it was happening again, the dreams ambushing me in daytime. I tried to wrench myself away, but it was too late. The window was gone and I was trapped inside the dream.

The sky was dark, the only colour the orange of flames. I thought for a moment that it was nighttime—which would have been good, night is the friend of firefighters—but then I saw that it was smoke filling the air.

From my knees down, my legs disappeared into dark pitchy smoke. The next layer of smoke was more yellow, resinous. The smoke around my head was whitish and furnace hot. It hurt to breathe.

I stood in the heart of the fire. The wind shrieked, and the flames roared over a hundred feet up into the air. The fire spread faster than I would have believed possible. Fiery debris and fireballs that size of baseballs flew through the air, igniting spot fires up ahead. The heat was intense.

Then I somehow moved through the fire to the wet line at the rear where the firefighters fought their grim war on the ground, battling with power saws, spades and pulaskis—a pole with a hoe on one end and an axe on the other. I recognized my dad wielding a rubber hose and pump that he carried on his back.

Off to his left stood a totem snag, the charred trunk of a giant spruce tree. As I watched, the tree started to topple and fall towards my dad.

"No!" I screamed.

The tree hesitated, halfway down.

"Oh yes. What you are seeing will happen." This time instead of coming from something in my dream like the black widow, the wulfdraigle's voice seemed to come from everywhere at once, to fill the sky. This must have been what Rex referred to as the "voice of thunder routine." I hadn't understood how terrifying it would be.

"Your father will die, unless—"

"Unless what?" I stalled, my eyes still glued to the tree.

"Unless you become a conduit."

Save my father at the price of watching Grantmere burn. Both choices were unacceptable; I didn't know what to do. The tree slipped down another foot. "Stop it! Stop it!" I yelled, putting my hands over my face.

"First your answer," the voice demanded. "Your family will be allowed to live if you become one of us."

I couldn't let Dad die. All my high-and-mighty ideals crumbled in front of the thought of him dead. Defeated, I opened my mouth to accept—and Lissa yelled in my ear, "No, Brianne! Don't!"

The noise was so loud I woke up and found myself back in my bed at home. But Lissa was still there, her pixie face wan and pale. "Don't do it! The wulfdraigles cheat. They'd make you a conduit, and then kill us anyway. Aunt Elise said so."

I tried to soothe her. "It's okay, Lissa. You woke me up in time. I didn't say yes, and Dad didn't die." Neither one of us asked what the other was talking about. We knew.

She calmed down enough for me to question her. "Did you say Aunt Elise?" She nodded. I stiffened. "But Aunt Elise is dead," I reminded her.

Lissa looked scornful. "I know *that*!"

"Then why—how—?" I didn't know how to frame the question.

"I asked her why she wasn't in heaven, and she said she hadn't gone yet because she was worried about us and she wanted to tone."

"Atone?" I guessed. For being a conduit and allowing the wulfdraigles evil to flow through her dreams.

"Yes." Lissa nodded. "She tried to warn you, but you were surrounded."

I shivered. The wulfdraigles had surrounded me. I was lucky Lissa had gotten through.

"She said for me to wake you up and give you her message right away."

"Which is?"

"That the wulfdraigles cheat." Fear crept back into Lissa's eyes. "You won't make a deal with them, will you?"

"Of course not." My words reassured Lissa, but did nothing to thaw the core of ice in my marrow.

chapter twelve

I woke to the shrill beeps of the fire alarm and the acrid smell of smoke. I jumped out of bed in a stuttering panic. Suzy was just sitting up, and I turned back and yanked her along with me.

Mom and Lissa met us in the hall. Mom sent us outside while she went back in to see where the fire was. The three of us huddled together on the driveway, probably not as far away as we should have been, but unwilling to get too far from Mom.

I looked for a black cloud of smoke coming from the house, but could see none. Instead the air seemed hazy everywhere. Smoky. Even before Mom motioned us back inside, I'd realized the truth: smoke from the forest fire had set off our alarm.

The wind had shifted.

We went inside and, even though it was only 6 AM, Mom turned on the radio. Sure enough, the Douglas Hills fire had come a lot closer during the night. It was now burning only 90 km away. Which sounded like a healthy distance until I remembered that an *average* fire moved about thirty 30 km/h. A health advisory was given that anyone with respiratory difficulties should keep indoors out of the smoke. "No evacuation order has yet been given, but all Grantmere schools are closed for the day because of the fire."

Even Lissa didn't cheer. Despite Dad's occupation, this was the closest a forest fire had come to touching our lives.

"I'm going back to bed," Suzy announced.

"I don't think that's a good idea," I said.

Mom looked worried. "You can lie down, if you'd like, but get dressed first. If we have to go, we may need to move fast."

I envied Suzy's ability to sleep at a time like this. After getting dressed and having breakfast, I didn't know what to do with myself. Lissa was colouring at the kitchen table, while Mom did dishes. I had homework, but knew I wouldn't be able to concentrate. My every nerve ending was screaming, "Do something! You've got to stop the fire!" Only I didn't know how.

At six-thirty, the report that I'd been dreading came on the radio.

"A new fire, probably caused by lightning, is blocking access to secondary highway No. 33 and the town of Grantmere. It is not—repeat NOT—safe to leave town using that highway. A blockade is in place, and only fire vehicles are allowed through."

Secondary highway No. 33 was the only highway out of town, with Grantmere sandwiched in the foothills the way it was.

"Since the Douglas Hill fire is also moving in on the town, priority is being given to putting out the highway fire. In the meantime, no evacuation order has yet been given, but Grantmere residents are advised to pack essential belongings and fuel up their cars. If you are unable to drive, phone the RCMP or a neighbour and arrangement will be made for you to be picked up. Keep tuned to this station for further details and instructions."

Mom turned down the radio, stared blankly at it, then roused herself. She looked suddenly older. "Well, it seems you were right after all, Brianne. There was lightning."

"Oh, have we stopped ignoring my dreams?" I asked snidely.

"Yes." Mom bowed her head. "I guess I always knew your dream was the true kind. I just didn't want to admit it."

I waited.

"I'm sorry, Brianne."

I blinked back tears. "I need to know that I can trust you. I need to know that you'll believe me if I tell you stuff." My voice came out raw.

Mom bit her lip. "You can trust me. I swear it. I may not like the fact that you have these dreams, but I won't play ostrich anymore." She held out her arms, and we hugged. Both of us were crying now, but not for long. There wasn't time.

Mom swiped at her eyes and pulled away. "Well, you heard the radio. There's no cause to panic yet. I'm going to go down to the fire department and see if they need help manning the phones in case of an evacuation. Wake up Suzy and pack some overnight clothes and keepsakes—keep it small—and load up the Green Machine. Keep the radio on. If the evacuation order is given, I want you girls to hop in the car and go—don't worry about me. Try to get a hotel room in Hinton." Mom gave me her credit card.

The thought of leaving without Mom terrified me, but I nodded.

"Before I go, is there anything else you need to tell me?"

She meant my dreams. I immediately remembered the heavy pine tree falling on Dad. My throat closed up. I *couldn't* worry her like that, when we had no way to warn Dad. Communicating in the middle of a fire fight was pretty spotty. And what if the ringing of the cellphone distracted him from the tree falling? No, best to leave things be. I reminded myself that Lissa had woken me before Dad was hurt. "No," I told Mom.

She left, and Lissa came out of her corner where she'd been listening, as quiet as a mouse. "Is this the real world, Brianne, or am I dreaming?"

"What?" I looked at her sharply, but Lissa just stared back with huge dark eyes. "The real world, of course."

With almost religious ceremony, Lissa pulled out the chain she wore around her neck and moved the charm—no, a button—to the front.

The waiting was getting to be too much for me. I got up. "Come on, we've got packing to do." I decided to let Suzy sleep a little longer, so we did Mom's room first, making several trips out to the car with photo albums. I decided to throw in the box of Aunt Elise's stuff, too. Then Lissa's room. I stuffed her teddy bear into her backpack with her nightgown and toothbrush. As I went down the hall to the room Suzy and I shared, my mind ticked along, planning what I would take. The disks with my stories, the afghan Mom had knitted me—

And then I saw Suzy's empty bed. "Where's Suzy?"

"I forgot to watch her." Lissa looked stricken.

The roar of a motor sent both of us running to the window, just in time to see the Green Machine back out of the garage.

"Suzy!" I yelled through the window screen.

She didn't look at me, although in straightening to go down the driveway, she drove almost underneath the window. "Suzy! Come back! We need the car in case the town's evacuated!"

She didn't stop, eyes focussed straight ahead—

"Oh, my God. She's sleepwalking. *Sleepdriving*. She's going to get herself killed!"

I took off out of the room at a run. The Green Machine was turning down the road to town when I got outside. She hadn't crashed. Yet.

I had no vehicle to follow her with. No vehicle to drive into town with. There was only my ten-speed bike. But how far could Suzy get, driving in her sleep? She was liable to crash into the first car she encountered, or drive into a ditch when she should turn....

I threw a leg over my bike, wheeling it off the grass and onto the driveway. "I'm going to follow Suzy," I told Lissa. Except I couldn't leave Lissa home alone with a forest fire approaching. "Grab your bike. You can stay at Czernick's." Lissa sometimes played with Mandy Czernick, Hayley's sister. Of course, their friendship pre-dated the news of my nefarious deed.

Wordlessly, Lissa ran for her bike. We pedaled the quarter mile to Czernick's together. I left her in the driveway. "Call Mom and tell her where you are. Tell her Suzy—" I stopped and changed my mind. Mom's concern would be all tied up in the approaching fire and Dad. She didn't need another problem. "No, don't." I might be wrong. Suzy might not be sleepwalking at all, might only have decided to go for a drive to get out of the house.

That explanation made a lot more sense. Of course, Suzy wasn't sleepwalking. How could somebody drive a car in her sleep?

Then again, was sleepdriving any weirder than sleeping while walking or putting on shoes?

I couldn't take the chance, and I was wasting time. "I'll be back as soon as I can," I told Lissa. "Will you be all right?"

Lissa's face was pale but resolute. "Yes. Hurry up and find Suzy before she falls."

I was a hundred meters down the road before the connection dawned on me. Lissa had asked me about a "fall girl" the night of Rex's phone call. Had she been talking about Suzy? I pedalled harder, but soon even Suzy's dust trail had vanished. I slowed down. It was four miles to town, and I had to conserve my strength.

I was out of breath and coasting by the time I passed the second mile. Since I'd gotten my driver's license, I hadn't biked as much, and I was out of shape. The smoke didn't help, clogging my lungs and making me want to cough. A hill loomed ahead, and I wasn't able to make it all the way up. I got off my bike and started pushing.

A blue car zoomed over the hill, missing me by inches. My heart was still pounding when I recognized Rex's blue sports car.

It zigged over and screeched to a halt within 150 metres. I watched in amazement: both his brakes and reaction time were incredibly swift. Then, totally ignoring the danger in the blindness of the curve, Rex backed up to where I stood. He was alone.

He didn't bother with greetings just barked out, "Where's Suzy?"

I didn't say a word, my glare reminding Rex, in case he had forgotten, that we were enemies. He worked for the wulfdraigles. Even if I'd known, I wouldn't have told him.

Rex got the message and swore impatiently. "Brianne! I don't have time for this. Suzy's in trouble, and I've got to find her!" His voice was hoarse. With a shock, I noticed his face was pale beneath his tan and his knuckles showed white on the steering wheel. "Where is she?" he demanded again.

I responded to the urgency in his voice. "She took off."

Rex's face showed despair, then he came to a lightning decision. "Get in the car."

"What?" I gaped.

"Get in!" Suppressed violence showed in Rex's face, telling me if I didn't get in, he'd throw me in. I hesitated.

He all but growled at me. "Just stop and think for a moment. We both know the town's about to go up in flames. The only safe place is Huxton's, which the fire will miraculously miss. Yet here I am out here, risking my butt. If I didn't care more for Suzy than I do for breathing, do you think I'd be here?"

Rex was right. He ought to be kicking back somewhere, not running around like a maniac. That and the panic in his voice convinced me.

I scrambled into the passenger seat.

chapter thirteen

Rex made a quick U-turn and accelerated before I'd closed the door. I fumbled for my seatbelt.

"Where are we going?" I had to yell over the throb of the motor.

"I don't know." Rex didn't look at me, and the car burned up the road. "We have to find Suzy before—" He broke off, but I completed his sentence in my head. Before the fire reached town.

I made a choice of my own then. Conduit or not Rex and I shared a common goal. "She's driving a twelve-year-old green Chrysler."

Rex nodded once. Within five minutes we hit Grantmere's town limits. Rex cut our speed and scanned cars with eagle eyes. "We've got to find her." Rex talked more to himself than me, his expression fierce. "We've got to keep her from falling asleep. Was she tired today? I bet the wulfdraigles kept her awake all night. They want her to do something for them in her sleep. We've got to—"

I felt sick. "It's too late. She's driving in her sleep."

Rex stared at me, aghast, for one moment then started scanning the street again. "Help me look."

No green cars on either Main or First Street. We turned down the avenue with Grantmere's post office.

"If anything happens to Suzy, I'll—I'll—" Rex broke off.

"Do what?" I asked, unimpressed. "Ask the wulfdraigles nicely not to do it again? That'll work. I mean, you're such a valuable employee, after all."

"No," Rex said. "I don't work for them anymore."

I made a rude noise. "Since when?"

"Since this morning. I wanted to see Suzy first thing, to warn her, but I got tied up in the mess with Sir Jeremy."

"What mess?" I asked.

"Stroke," Rex said, eyes searching ahead.

I gasped, outraged. "You call an old man's stroke a mess? He's your guardian!"

"No, he isn't."

So Rex was a sponger. My temper flared. "Guardian or not he's still a human being!"

"Is he?" Rex asked oddly, his mouth twisted. "He doesn't deserve the title. He's a coward and a murderer, not to mention crazy. He's the conduit that shot your aunt." Rex looked defiant, as if he didn't expect me to believe him—which made me think he was telling the truth. Sir Jeremy had killed Aunt Elise.

Pain stabbed me. My mind raced even as I kept searching for the Green Machine. "And Chris? Ben's brother?"

Rex slanted a glance at me. "Yes. When did you figure that out? I wanted to strangle you when you let Sir Jeremy see Ben. I went to a lot of trouble to keep the fact that his witness had an identical twin from Sir Jeremy." He turned down a side street. We were in the residential area now.

I felt cold. "You knew it had to have been Chris because Chris was dating Hayley. But if Sir Jeremy had known about Ben, he wouldn't have wanted to take the chance that he'd gotten the wrong twin." I remembered how Sir Jeremy had talked about ghosts when he saw Ben.

"Yes. You're lucky Sir Jeremy didn't make an attempt on Ben's life afterward," Rex said.

"Not that lucky," I said. "He did make an attempt. Someone put a black widow spider in Ben's pickup yesterday. He had to go to the hospital."

"Damn it!" Rex pounded on the steering wheel. "So that's where he disappeared to yesterday. I should have known he was up to something. He almost never leaves the house these days."

"Will he try again?" I asked. "How serious was his stroke?"

"I don't know. I think his stroke was an arranged distraction on the wulfdraigles' part to keep me from talking to Suzy. Which doesn't mean he won't croak. At his age, any health problem is deadly, and from the wulfdraigles' point of view he's just about outlived his usefulness. That's why they had me living with him as his 'ward', so I could step in and do the grunt tasks if needed."

I glared at him. "Like dealing with me."

"Oh, no," Rex said. The mockery I hated was back in his eyes. "Sorry to blow your ego, but Suzy was always more important than you. You were just a complication. They told me to gain Suzy's trust and to either recruit you or make sure no one would believe you if you started blabbing about your dreams—especially not your sister. They need Suzy for something. Something big."

"What?"

"I don't know, but if Suzy is sleepdriving, then it's happening right now. We have to stop her, if we can. Save her."

I struggled to make sense of it all. "What do the wulfdraigles want with a sleepwalker?"

"Sleepwalkers are highly vulnerable to wulfdraigle-sent dreams. They react to them as if they're real while they're dreaming. It has something to do with their level of consciousness."

Suzy was in danger... But. "But why do they want to send her dreams? I mean, they already have conduits to do their bidding."

"True. Us conduits will do almost anything the wulfdraigles ask of us." He paused. "Almost. We won't go on suicide missions."

"And sleepwalkers will?" My voice was shrill.

"She'll be walking in a dream world. She'll only see what the wulfdraigles want her to see. She'll be blind to the danger."

Oh, God.

"If I could just figure out what they need her for, we might be able to find her. Damn it," Rex said in frustration. He finished cruising down the street, turned left and headed down the next street.

I looked at my watch. Twenty minutes had now passed since Suzy took off. This was a waste of time. Rex's plan wasn't working.

I stilled. Somehow, in the panic over Suzy's disappearance, I had forgotten one crucial fact. Rex was a conduit. What if Rex's contrition was all just an act, a way to stall me and keep me from finding Suzy?

As we slowed for the next corner, I surreptitiously put my fingers on the door handle. Should I jump?

"I thought I'd fooled them, you know," Rex said, his voice bitter and self-derisive. "I really thought they didn't know—how I felt about Suzy."

"And how *do* you feel?" I asked.

"I'm in love with her," Rex said.

There was something soft and wondering in his expression, but I hardened my heart. Rex had been using Suzy as a subtle threat to me since the beginning. "And when did you come to this realization?" I asked.

"The day I came to your house. It blew me away when she gave that big speech, you know. Your sister actually likes *me*. Up until then I'd been pretending that Suzy was just another girl. Last year I dated Tillie Gerard. She liked the presents I gave her and being seen with me, but she didn't actually like spending time alone with me. Suzy does. Did. I had fun with her. I'd forgotten what fun was. But now she hates me. The wulfdraigles made sure of that."

I suddenly realized Rex was no fonder of the wulfdraigles than I was. I took my hand off the door handle.

I remembered him saying he had been normal once; impulsively, I asked, "How did you become a conduit?"

Rex flashed me a dazzling smile. "Me? I was easy to catch. Greed. Plain greed." He turned haunted eyes in my direction. "You wouldn't understand. I grew up in the slums. No father, an alcoholic for a mother. We lived on welfare and struggled to eat. The only thing I cared for on earth besides my own skin was my brother. Mark. We went everywhere together. He was the skinniest little kid you'd ever seen. He got beat-up a lot at school." Rex's hands clenched into fists. "God, I hated them for that. If a rich kid got beat-up, the bullies would have been expelled. But all they got was a lecture."

Rex paused. When he continued, it was as if I was no longer there, so lost was he in old memories. "The dream was so wonderful. Money, cars, power, everything. How could I not wish for it? It was everything I wanted." He gave a short bitter laugh. "Nobody can say the wulfdraigles aren't good at their job.

"I saved a little girl from getting hit by a car; my name got in the papers. Then Sir Jeremy showed up, saying how he'd been in love with my grandmother and wanted to do something for her grandsons. He bought me a car, gave us gifts. Suddenly we had money, and when my mother OD'd Sir Jeremy stepped in as our guardian. We sent Mark off to one of those expensive private schools.

"Then the nightmares started—people screaming, dying. It took three dreams for me to catch on, and even then I found it hard to believe. It was too unreal, but they kept coming, dream after dream, too many to be coincidence. I got scared. Really scared."

"Wasn't there something you could do?" I asked unthinkingly. Fat lot I'd been able to do a year ago in Edmonton. Or now.

"Oh, sure." Rex's voice was hard. "I used to rush around like a chicken with its head cut off warning people just like you do. Until I realized I was only helping the wulfdraigles. I'd dream of things and inform the police. They would laugh and say, 'Run along, kid.' They never did anything to stop it." His hands fisted. "Then when it happened they'd start looking at me strangely and asking where I had been at such and such a time."

Rex's voice became heavy and reluctant. "One day I dreamed Mark had an accident at school. I drove like a maniac, but I was too late. The ambulance was driving away when I arrived.

"Sir Jeremy arrived and put his hand on my shoulder, but his eyes were oh, so cold. He said it was a shame about my brother, only I could tell he didn't mean it. Then he said there were ways to protect the people you loved. Mark didn't have to die.

"I had been barely listening before, but when he mentioned dreams I looked up. I'll never forget his expression, the power in his face. He repeated that my brother didn't have to die, but I had to stop fighting the true dreams the wulfdraigles sent me and obey the directions they gave me in my dreams. So I became a conduit; Mark didn't die, and everything was fine. For a while."

I remembered the words Lissa had woken me with the night I had been offered a deal. "The wulfdraigles cheat."

Rex glanced at me. "Yeah, that's right. They cheat. Mark didn't die, but I lost him anyway. Two years later he was hooked on drugs. He stole my car, cleaned me out of cash and left. My brother. I haven't seen him since."

"So why didn't you quit then?" I asked.

"Quit and do what?" Rex smiled humourlessly. "My money was gone. There was nobody under the sun I cared for other than myself. They rely a good bit on bribes. Cars, money, the handsome mask of a face.... I used to have terrible acne. When I started working for the wulfdraigles I had a dream about looking like a movie star and the next morning the acne was gone. Poof, just like that. Over the next few weeks my crooked teeth straightened out and my hair got several shades lighter. And if bribes don't work, they bring on the threats. They've got enough blackmail on me—most of it made up, some of it just true enough to be believable—to put me in jail for years."

I shivered. "What now?"

Rex came back to life. "Now we find Suzy. When the wulfdraigles want something to happen in our world, they shape a dream of it and send it to one of their conduits. But because the dreamline is thinner around true dreamers, even dreams they don't want you to see leak through. Kind of like eavesdropping. Believe me, the wulfdraigles are very annoyed that you know about the fire—that you saw dreams intended only for Sir Jeremy and me. If they could block you out, they would have. Which means what's happening to Suzy should have shown up in our dreams in some form or another. What dreams of yours haven't come true yet besides the fire?"

"The empty reservoir," I said after a moment's thought. "It was full when Ben dived in."

"Yeah, I think I had that one too. I remember a huge muddy hole in the ground anyway. But I don't remember Suzy being there, do you?"

"I don't remember any dreams about Suzy."

"I had one that might have been her." Rex frowned. "It was dark, and I could only see her from the back. We were underground somewhere. Maybe in an unfinished basement or a tunnel, but I don't know where." He pounded the steering wheel in frustration. "I don't know Grantmere well enough."

"Me neither," I started to say then broke off. A thought clicked in. Tunnels. Ben's voice trying to soothe me after school yesterday, reciting his speech about— "The coal-mine. That's it!"

"Do you know where it is?"

"Not exactly. West of town, I think."

Rex turned left onto the highway and floored it.

"Stop! We need to ask for directions."

"Too late." Rex's smile did not quite mask his fear. "We'll just have to go with blind luck."

I fell silent and scanned the side roads for the Green Machine or a sign for the coal mine. Nothing, nothing and more nothing.

When we were about four kilometers out of town there was a sudden loud flapping noise, and the car veered left into the oncoming lane. I screamed at Rex; an approaching van blared its horn; Rex spun the wheel hard to the right.

In less time than it took to sneeze we hit the ditch on the right-hand side of the road. My seatbelt jerked tight against my chest, bruising me, and an airbag went off in my face.

When I fought my way out of the white cloud, Rex was swearing. "Are you hurt?" I yelled.

He neither answered nor stopped cursing, but he undid his seatbelt and jumped out of the car so I figured he must be okay. I checked my own body with trembling hands and decided that I probably was, too. Adrenaline crashed through my body. It took me five tries to undo my seatbelt and longer to understand what had happened. When I finally made it out into the ditch with Rex, I saw the flat driver's side tire.

"Do you have a spare?" I asked. The van hadn't stopped. I tried not to think too badly of the driver; the encroaching forest fire probably had a lot of people panicked.

Wordlessly, Rex popped the trunk. The spare tire was there, but the rubber was shredded as if someone had gone after it with a knife.

"They know," Rex said hollowly. "*They know.*"

"Who? The wulfdraigles?"

A nod. "They know I've defected. They detest traitors; they must have instructed Sir Jeremy to sabotage the tires. I should have been suspicious when I found him collapsed on the floor of the garage. There was no reason for him to be there. I should have taken his Volvo, but all I thought about was speed."

Rex took out his cellphone, but soon made a sound of frustration. "The batteries are missing."

"What do we do?"

"We get another car."

There was an ugly light in Rex's eyes that I didn't like. Somehow "get" sounded more like "steal." But now wasn't the time to argue. Rex started to run back towards town, and I followed at a jog, wishing I still had my bike, but, of course, it wouldn't have fit in Rex's stupid teeny tiny sports car.

After only a few minutes a stitch in my side forced me to slow to a walk.

A huge plume of smoke rose ominously in the distance. How close was the forest fire? How much time did we even have?

I broke into a run again. Within two strides the stitch in my side returned, and I was soon panting, hot and sweaty. Rex was almost half a mile ahead of me when I heard a vehicle coming.

I staggered out onto the middle of the road and waved my arms, determined. The driver would either have to stop, or run me down.

chapter fourteen

Even before the pickup screeched to a stop, I recognized the driver.

"Ben!" My smile almost split my face. "I'm so glad to see you!" I hurried around to the passenger side of the pickup. Now we had a chance of finding Suzy before the flames arrived.

"No doubt." Ben unlocked the door for me, and I scrambled inside. "What are you doing out here, anyway? Don't you know the town's being evacuated? I couldn't believe it when your sister phoned and said you were running around out here on foot."

"My sister?" I said sharply. "Suzy?" I hardly dared hope.

"Nope, Lissa," Ben replied.

"I need to get to the coal mine," I told Ben. "Suzy's there. She's in trouble."

Ben looked uneasy. "Jeez, there's not much time before the fire gets here. Are you sure she's at the mine? Why would she go there?"

"The wulfdraigles sent her. She's sleepwalking," I said baldly. I didn't have time to come up with a convincing half-truth, no matter how crazy the true explanation sounded.

"How could she sleepwalk to the mine?" Ben asked.

He didn't believe me. That was my cue to get angry and stamp off, but this time I didn't have time for bruised feelings. "She's in danger. Will you help, or should I flag down another car?"

Ben sighed. "Of course, I'll help you. Besides, I'm not sure anyone else will stop. The town's in a panic. They—" He broke off, his gaze on the side of the road. His jaw tightened. "What's *he* doing here?"

I looked and sure enough Rex had turned around and was running back towards us.

Ben scowled as Rex got closer. Of course. The last time we had talked, I had sworn Rex terrified me and we were enemies. "Oh, you mean Rex," I said lamely. How to explain?

Rex reached for the door—and Ben engaged the auto-lock. He pounded on the window. "Let me in!"

"Not a chance." Ben started to drive on the shoulder.

"Hey!" Rex ran alongside, holding to the side mirror. "Brianne, make him stop."

I felt somewhat bemused. "Are you really going to leave him here with a forest fire coming?"

"He murdered Chris."

I winced. I'd forgotten I'd confided that little suspicion to Ben.

Ben had the pickup up to 25 km/h now, and Rex was barely hanging on, his face red. I took a moment to savour; payback was sweet.

But I might yet need his help to save Suzy. I put my hand over Ben's. "Stop. He didn't kill Chris. I was wrong."

Ben eased off the gas. "What?"

"He's switched sides. He's helping us now."

"You swear he didn't run Chris down?"

"I swear."

Ben stopped the pickup and unlocked the door. Rex swung himself inside, red-faced and gasping. Without a word, Ben pulled back out onto the highway.

"How far to the mine?" I asked.

"Not far. Five minutes drive, maybe."

Rex recovered his breath enough to gasp out. "Can't this—thing—go any—faster?" He was thinking of Suzy, but he sounded very rude.

Ben looked on the verge of saying something ugly, and I touched his arm. "Please, Ben. I know you don't like to speed, but this is an emergency."

Ben gave a short nod, and then increased our speed to 115 km/h.

Rex made a sound of disgust, but Ben ignored him. In desperation I turned on the radio.

The news was all bad. The highway fire was still blocking the road out of town and the Douglas Hills fire was raging closer. I felt sick. My eyes were drawn again to the black tower of smoke on my left.

For a while the only noise was the rattle of the engine.

To my surprise, Ben took the same road that we'd taken to the reservoir, only he turned off of it about a mile before and headed up a foothill. Most of the road ran through trees, but when we came out into a clearing, we could look down and see the reservoir. I was heartened to see three water trucks filling up.

"Here we are," Ben said as we came around the last switchback.

My throat tightened; the Green Machine was parked by the mine entrance. Rex looked questioningly at me, and I nodded. "That's our car." I looked at my watch and realized it had been forty minutes since Suzy drove off.

We parked next to the mine entrance and got out. "Suzy!" I called. "It's Brianne. Where are you?"

No answer. I called a couple more times before taking a closer look at the mine entrance. It was obviously abandoned and held the grunge of years. A big spider web hung stretched across one corner, and I shuddered. Under normal circumstances, I couldn't envision Suzy entering such a place. Was she still sleepwalking?

Rex was already moving inside, calling her name, but I hesitated. It was so dark in there. A person could easily fall down a shaft to their death. "Do you have a flashlight?" I asked Ben.

"I think so." Ben went over to his pickup and searched under the seat. In a minute he came back with one and switched it on. "Well, it works," Ben said doubtfully. "But I can't vouch for the batteries."

The flashlight beam, pale in the sunlight, helped a good deal in the dark of the mine. It revealed a rather low rock ceiling supported by old timbers. A sign not far in declared the mine UNSAFE: Authorized Personnel Only.

"She's not here," Rex said despairingly. "The tunnel ends about forty feet in."

Ben snorted. Rex narrowed his eyes, and Ben explained. "What we're in now is only a small part of the mine. There's a shaft going down about a hundred feet and more tunnels at the bottom."

"Then we'll need an elevator," I said quickly. I looked hopefully at Ben. "Do you know...?"

"This way." Ben swung the flashlight beam at the far wall and walked toward a metal railing. He stopped there, staring down a deep shaft, his eyebrows rising in surprise. "Somebody *is* down there. The elevator's usually left at the top." He pulled on one of the ropes, and, with Rex's help, hauled the elevator up to our level.

The elevator was nothing more than a small wire cage, and I was the last one to enter it. "Is it safe?" I asked doubtfully. I hung on tight to the wire mesh wall.

Even in the dim glow of the flashlight, I could see Ben's smile. "They used this to haul coal, Brianne. I think it'll support the three of us."

Ben and Rex began the tedious process of lowering us down the shaft while I held the flashlight. Every once in a while we would pass a blank wall with the level number painted on it, but no tunnels.

Ben saw my glance and explained, "There's only one working floor down on the very bottom where the coal was. That's level six."

"How do you know so much, Harper?" Rex's voice thrummed with tension. I knew he was just worried about Suzy and was trying to get his mind off of it, but Ben took the words as a personal criticism.

"I did a project on coal mines, featuring the Grantmere collier, and got a conducted tour," Ben said stiffly.

The number "6" appeared, and we hit solid ground. I left the elevator gratefully, but the feeling faded once I had a look around. Other than the narrow flashlight beam, the place was as dark and silent as a tomb. Suzy was down here? "Suzy?" I called her name. It echoed hollowly.

"Suzy?" Rex took up the call, moving around the outer limits of the room we were in.

I shivered from the draft caused by the air shaft on my right. Ben moved the flashlight, and I stared, appalled, at all the tunnels branching out. "How far down are we?" Fear flattened my voice.

"About one hundred feet," Ben told me cheerfully. "The coal bed had more width than depth which is why there are so many tunnels. The place is like a honeycomb."

The dread in me increased, and my voice sharpened as I yelled, "Suzy! It's Brianne. Please answer me!" I motioned Rex into silence, waiting for a reply, and crossed my fingers. Please, Suzy, I begged silently, wake up.

I strained my eyes down several possible passageways. Coal dust lay thick everywhere. In the third tunnel, I noticed the imprint of a pair of running shoes. "Suzy," I said, voice light with relief. "She went this way."

Ben and Rex hurried over, and we followed the footprints, occasionally calling Suzy's name.

We found her about three hundred feet down the tunnel.

The flashlight almost passed over her without pausing, her face and hair were so streaked with coal dust. She crouched against one wall, ceaselessly moving something in her hands. It made a small clicking sound.

"Suzy?" I ran the last few steps and peered into her eyes. They were frighteningly blank. She did not see me. The clicking sound continued. I shook her shoulders, no response. "She's still asleep," I told Ben and Rex. "Last time she didn't wake up until I pinched her."

"Don't," Rex said. He moved forward beside me. "Let me try." Gently, his hands closed over hers, and the clicking sound stopped. He kissed her.

At first she didn't respond, then she gave a little shiver and kissed him back. For an instant. Then her eyes opened and she remembered she was angry with him. She pushed him away. "What are you doing here?" She looked around with wide eyes and saw Ben and me. "Where the hell are we?"

"The coal mine." I stepped forward. "You've been sleepwalking."

Suzy frowned. "But the coal mine's on the other side of town. How could I have walked that far?"

"You didn't. You drove. Sleptdrove."

Suzy kept shaking her head, denying it.

"It's true," I insisted. "Remember the other times you went sleepwalking? You were heading for the car both times. This time I didn't get to you in time."

"That's impossible," Suzy said flatly.

"It's true," Rex said.

Her attention switched back to him and, with it, her anger. Her scornful laugh rang out. "And I'm supposed to believe you? After all the other times you lied?"

Rex flushed, something I had never seen him do before. I started to say something, but Rex interrupted. "It doesn't matter. Now that I know you're safe, I'll wait a little farther down the tunnel while you guys talk." His eyes were soft as they rested on Suzy, and his voice, compared to all the other times I'd heard it heaping abuse and oozing sarcasm, sounded amazingly gentle.

"Good!" Suzy threw the word at his retreating back, but I knew her well enough to sense her hurt. She had trusted Rex, and he had failed her.

"Suzy!" I reprimanded.

"What?" She glared at me as if I'd turned traitor on her—which in a way I had—and I felt worse than ever.

Ben stepped between us. "What have you got there?" He shone the flashlight on Suzy's hand, and she opened it to reveal something like a thermostat with the cover off. A wire snaked from it to the ground before disappearing in the darkness.

"I don't know," Suzy said. "I was dreaming about flicking on a light switch."

"It's a switch, all right. A mercury switch," Ben murmured. "They used them to trigger explosions farther down the tunnel. A few probably got left over by accident. Good thing none of them are still connected." He smiled. "Otherwise the whole mine would have collapsed around you."

The mercury switch looked connected to me—there were wires coming out of it—and Suzy had to have been down here for at least half an hour. Long enough to do other things in her sleep.

Everything became clear then. Suzy's importance to the wulfdraigles' scheme, my dream of the empty reservoir, the fire, and the labyrinth of tunnels. "Oh, my God," I whispered. Ben and Suzy turned to look at me, but if I was right there was no time to explain. "Run for the elevator!" I yelled.

We had barely gotten five steps when an explosion shook the tunnel. I lost my balance and fell. Small rocks and dirt rained down on me. I covered my face against it, but the tunnel did not collapse.

Then it was over, and Ben was helping me to my feet. The flashlight had fallen to the ground and provided only a dim glow.

"Suzy?" Rex called and stumbled into our midst.

Suzy shook off his hands. "I'm fine."

"Come on," I interrupted. "We have to get out of here."

Ben scooped up the flashlight. "Yeah. Let's not wait around for a cave-in."

"Forget the cave-in," I said. "Do you hear that rumbling noise? Do you know what that is? The explosion cracked the reservoir floor. In another few minutes we're going to be drowning! Run!"

chapter fifteen

We ran. The flashlight beam bounced along. Twice I stumbled over debris fallen from the tunnel roof. The second time Suzy gave a sharp cry. "I twisted my ankle," she yelled above the growing roar.

"Lean on me," Rex yelled. For once Suzy didn't argue, and we limped along at a slower pace.

The first rivulet of water swept along past our feet, gleaming black in the dim light. There was a muffled crash, no doubt more of the tunnel ceiling collapsing under the pressure of the reservoir water. The roar increased.

I ran back, sliding in the mud, to put Suzy's other arm around my shoulder. "Hurry," I yelled. I doubt anyone heard me, but it didn't matter. We were travelling as fast as we could.

A wave of water hit us in the back of the knees, causing us to stagger. Suzy fell, but Rex and I hauled her to her feet and kept running. The water dropped back to mid-calf, but I knew it would keep rising. I kept sight of Ben's bobbing flashlight ahead and tried to run faster. It was hard to find purchase on the floor, but the current helped to sweep us forward.

More water poured in, swirling around our knees. Gasping, and crying in fright, we struggled forward, only to almost plow

Ben down. He stood at a fork in the tunnels. "The footprints are gone," he yelled.

I hadn't thought it was possible to get any more frightened, but it was. I hadn't paid much attention to our route on the way. One wrong turn and we would be lost in the tunnels forever. No, not forever. We would drown long before then.

Rex didn't even pause. "This way!" He turned left. Suzy and I splashed along with him. The water now reached up to mid-thigh.

The next wave hit me just below the shoulder, knocking me down and tearing me away from Suzy. I swallowed water and flailed desperately with my arms. I reached the surface, gasping, and found myself in total darkness being swept forward with the current.

I screamed and heard someone else shouting, but in the echo-filled darkness couldn't get a fix on it. The force of the water slammed me into a wall, then spun me around, before I could get any purchase. I yelled again and swallowed water.

The current pulled me on. I struggled to keep my head above water. I was a poor swimmer at best, and the wild, dark water sapped my strength, its cold seeping into my bones.

I tried to swim forward, and one hand scraped the dirt ceiling. Very soon the water would fill the tunnel.

Then the ceiling abruptly got higher. Was the water going down, or had I entered a bigger chamber?

"Brianne!" someone called. "Over here!"

I struck out toward the noise, but the current fought me, and I made little progress. I finally came in contact with a wall and used it to pull myself along.

"Over here!" someone called. They were closer this time. "I found the elevator."

Hope returned, and I found the courage to push off from the wall toward a faint gray spot. The current grabbed me again. "No!" I cried just before someone's fingers caught my wrist.

I clung tightly to that lifeline and kicked my legs. Slowly, I was pulled forward until my other hand brushed wire mesh. I hooked my fingers into the elevator cage, pulling myself inside.

"Brianne, are you okay?" Ben's voice. Ben's strong hand holding mine.

"Yes," I gasped. "Suzy? Rex?"

"Both here," Ben shouted. "But your sister's unconscious. Rex is holding her head above water. We have to hurry!"

A nightmare moment of searching in the dark and water for the ropes, and then we both pulled on them. The water weighted the cage down, and at first I thought I wouldn't be able to do it. My muscles were already aching from swimming in the cold water and bruised from being slammed into tunnel walls.

Then the rope moved, and the water poured out. I placed my hands higher on the rope and pulled again. I gasped and my arm muscles soon shook from the effort. It took forever. When we cleared the water, Rex took over my place. I sat down on the elevator cage, unable to stand.

My fingers felt for Suzy and touched damp strands of hair. I lifted her head onto my lap and put my hand under her nose to make sure she was breathing.

The roar of water below us gradually got fainter and the gray light above brighter. Suzy regained consciousness just before we reached the top. She groaned. "What happened?"

"It's all right," I said over and over. My voice shook. "We're safe. We're safe."

Once at the top, none of us could bear to remain in the coal mine, and we stumbled outside. Even the smoke-hazed sunlight seemed bright after the eternal night of the cave.

Wind touched my muddy clothing, and I shivered. Once I started, I couldn't stop. Wordlessly, Ben moved over beside me and put his arm around me. He wasn't any warmer than I was, but I snuggled closer anyhow. He had saved me from the current.

"You saved my life," Suzy said to Rex. Her eyes were wary.

Rex shrugged. "And Ben saved all three of us. Not that it really matters. We're all going to die in the fire anyhow."

The fire. I sat up straighter. "We have to stop it."

"Dad and the other firefighters will save the town," Suzy protested automatically. "The water in the reservoir—" she broke off.

"Is going down the drain," Rex finished. "Look!"

Shakily, I got to my feet, and we all walked over to the ridge overlooking the reservoir. The water level had dropped fifteen metres, and a huge whirlpool had formed near the center. Like an enormous gaping mouth, it swallowed up the last of the water, exposing the cracked hole caused by the explosion. The water trucks' hydrants were left dangling in mid-air.

Half a million tonnes of water just vanished.

"It's my fault," Suzy whispered. Her eyes rounded with horror.

"No, it's not!" Rex beat me to the protest. "It's the wulf-draigles' fault. You were just a tool. They took advantage of your sleepwalking. You didn't do anything."

His face was pale, and it struck me suddenly that his fabulous good looks had faded over the last few hours. It wasn't just mud that made the shining blond hair and white teeth seem duller, less perfect. I would bet money that a conduit somewhere had had a dream of Rex looking uglier.

"Don't even think about confessing," Rex added. "If they need someone to take the blame, it will be me."

"No," I said. "No confessions. No letting the wulfdraigles win. No one but us four know we were here and all the evidence just got washed away. Agreed?" I looked at everyone fiercely, until they each nodded.

Delicate white filaments began to drop from the sky.

Ben brushed one off his arms. "It's not snowing?" he asked incredulously.

"No," I said starkly. "It's ashes. From the fire."

It seemed a particularly bad omen. We needed rain, not ash.

"What now?" Ben asked.

Nobody said anything for a moment. There weren't a lot of options. We would just have to wait and hope that the highway fire subsided enough for people to drive out. The water already in the water trucks would be used to wet down roofs, but the inferno I'd dreamed of last night would dry them again almost instantly. Grantmere would be ashes by dawn.

Suzy broke the silence. "I'm going to go see what I can do to help fight the fire. The town will need every pair of hands they can get."

"I'll come with you," Rex volunteered. Suzy looked mutinous, but Rex cut her off, "You can't drive with a bump on your head." They headed for the Green Machine.

Ben was of the same mind, and within minutes we were on the road into town. He turned on the radio, and we listened in silence to the bulletins about the fire. It was now only sixteen kilometers to the northeast and moving fast. The secondary highway still hadn't been reopened, but people had started to drive out anyway, panicked, and traffic was backed up for miles.

The news tightened Ben's face and he turned to me. "I owe you an apology. You were right about the fire and the empty reservoir. I should have trusted you."

I didn't say to forget about it, because his lack of trust had hurt, but I did understand why he'd had a hard time believing me. "Apology accepted."

"Thanks." Ben let out his breath. "I promise next time, I'll listen."

I nodded and didn't say the truth—that there might not be a next time. That we might die today.

Smoke fogged the town, and more ashes dropped from the sky. Ben had to turn on the windshield wipers. The scenery flashed by, the trees green but already sickly looking from the gray cinders. All too soon, I feared, they would be blackened sticks.

"Lissa." I turned wide eyes on Ben. "I forgot all about Lissa. She's at Czernick's, but she'll be scared."

"No problem." Ben switched lanes smoothly, but the speedometer needle crept over the speed limit again.

Lissa was waiting by the door when we got there. I got a lecture from Mrs. Czernick for not telling her I was leaving Lissa and running off, but the need to evacuate her own family kept it fairly brief.

Once we were back in Ben's truck, a thought struck me. "Lissa, how did you know to call Ben?"

"Aunt Elise told me to," Lissa said as if it were the most commonplace thing in the world. "She likes Ben. She says he's got a good head on his shoulders."

Ben blinked, but said nothing.

I was absurdly pleased by the compliment from a ghost—and a former conduit at that.

"Okay, let's go," I said. "I'll call Mom and tell her we're with Ben. Ben, you should call your parents, too."

Lissa shook her head. "No. I don't want the town to burn down."

"Neither do I," I said. "It's not like we have a choice, though."

"Yes, you do." Lissa's dark eyes were unblinking. "You can make it rain. If it rains in your dream, it will rain here, and the fire will stop."

"And how am I supposed to make myself dream about rain?" I snapped.

"Actually," Ben said, an arrested look on his face, "that might not be as impossible as it sounds."

"What do you mean?" I asked him.

"You know how sometimes when your alarm goes off, your subconscious interprets it as a phone ringing in your dream so you don't wake up?"

I nodded.

"What if you heard water sounds, like someone taking a shower? You might dream it was raining."

I caught my breath. "It might work," I said, just as Ben changed his mind.

"Never mind—it's a crazy idea."

"No crazier than believing dreams come true," I said. "But it's worth a shot. If they don't reopen the highway soon, a lot of people might die." Including the three of us.

Ben took a deep breath. "Okay, we'll try." He drove back to our house, and we all hopped out. "You lie down and go to sleep. Lissa and I will handle the water noises. And if the fire gets too close or the highway opens, we'll wake you."

"Okay." But first I went and took some of the nighttime cold medication Mom kept on hand in the bathroom that warned about causing drowsiness.

I settled myself in Dad's padded easy chair, put the footrest up, tipped it back and closed my eyes. No go. I kept my eyes closed until I was sure at least fifteen minutes had passed, then opened them to see that only five minutes had passed. I sighed. "This isn't working."

"You're not relaxed," Ben admonished me. "Breathe deeply."

I tried, but just ended up counting my breaths. The smell of smoke hung in the air, and the only visions I had were of the fire racing through the forest until the flames licked hungrily at the town. I opened my eyes wide. What if I dreamt of the fire instead of the rain?

"It's no good," I told Ben, near tears. "I couldn't go to sleep if my life depended on it." Bad choice of words.

"Sure you can. Going to sleep is the easiest thing in the world," he soothed. "How about a lullaby?" he suggested, a spark of desperation in his eyes. "That's how my Mom used to put me and Chris to sleep." He sang softly, "Rockabye baby, in the treetop...."

I giggled. I couldn't help it. The whole thing was totally unreal. The town was about to burn up, and Benjamin Harper was singing me to sleep! It defied the imagination. My giggles turned into laughter, and I started hiccuping.

Ben looked at me in concern. "Hey, don't go hysterical on me now."

I tried to stop laughing, but couldn't and the shock of realizing it cured me of both the laughter and the hiccups. I closed my eyes in embarrassment and kept them closed.

To their credit, Ben and Lissa were very quiet. The other noises of the house seemed suddenly very loud by comparison. The gentle sound of water falling came to my ears, and I opened my eyes. "I'm not asleep yet—" My words died on my lips. The sound was not the shower going. It was raining.

I ran outdoors, laughing and shouting, and felt the rain beat down. It was a heavy downpour, not a shower. A light drizzle would have been worse than no rain at all—a fire could extract oxygen from it and burn harder. I called for Ben and Lissa, but they didn't come and, with a shock, I realized it was because I was asleep. The rain was a dream.

My joy didn't fade. It made no difference if it rained here or in the real world. If it did in one, it would in the other. I couldn't lose.

I danced a little, acting silly and even singing at the top of my lungs. It was just as well that Ben couldn't see me; he'd think I'd flipped out.

Thinking of Ben made me want to go back to the real world where he was. Time to wake up. I went back inside and repositioned myself on the chair, opening and closing my eyes several times. I wasn't sure how to go about waking up, but this seemed as good a way as any.

It worked. The line dividing the two worlds appeared, one gradually superimposing itself over the other. I could see Ben's face and saw from the exultation on it that it must be raining there, too.

Just as Ben's mouth formed the words, "She's waking up!" a strong hand grabbed me and pulled me away from the line. Back into the dream. Ben's face faded, and a little cry escaped my lips. I struggled and kicked.

But the hand still held me, and I looked up into the insane eyes of Sir Jeremy. He bared his teeth in what was meant to be a smile and spoke, his voice soft with menace, "Well, well. If it isn't the little do-gooder. Meddling again, I see."

chapter sixteen

"Aren't you supposed to be in the hospital?" I asked him.

"I died."

"Don't you mean the wulfdraigles killed you? Just because it was convenient?" I lashed out.

Sir Jeremy smiled thinly, but didn't rise to the bait. "That body was old. But the wulfdraigles long ago promised me sanctuary here from Hell's eternal fires when my time to die came. If the wulfdraigles can exist for millennia in the world of dreams, I suspect I should be good for a few centuries at least. If I need to wait that long. The wulfdraigles are very close to breaking free, and if they conjure physical bodies for themselves, why not me?"

"That's not going to happen," I told him. "It's raining. Your little fire is going to sputter and go out, and the wulfdraigles' plans will die with it."

He just smiled. "Is that so?" In the dream he was much stronger than a seventy-year-old man should be, and he dragged me over to the window. "Look outside," he commanded, gloating. "Does that look like rain to you?"

The rain had stopped. I'd failed.

No! As long as I was still dreaming there was a chance I could make the rain come back.

"It's not going to rain, Brianne. You'll have to kill me first."

I blinked, and Sir Jeremy mutated into the horse-sized black widow spider I had faced in Science class.

I didn't scream. I refused to give it the satisfaction. It advanced rapidly on all eight hairy legs, and I scrambled backward, calculating my chances against it. On the plus side I was more agile than it was. I knew the house better. On the minus side, it could capture me with its sticky web, kill me with venom and then suck out my dissolved body fluids leaving behind a dried husk. And I—I needed a weapon. Quick.

With a sudden change of direction, I scampered for the kitchen. The spider lunged for me, but missed, and I grabbed a butcher knife out of the wooden block by the sink. The spider started to squeeze through the door, but I held it back, brandishing my knife. "Get back!"

The spider hesitated, then backed up. "Fine," it said in an oily voice. "I'll just wait for the fire to burn you up. This is your last dream, Brianne. You won't be able to dream anymore because you'll be dead."

And there I was—stuck. Safe from the spider, but trapped by the need for rain. I attempted to sneak through to another room to attack it from behind, but I ended up in the hall while it took up position in the kitchen. Stalemate.

"Brianne!" I recognized Ben's voice, coming from the living room. "Where are you?"

The spider heard Ben, too, and we both made a dash for the living room. I made it there first, barely. The spider's cephalothorax filled the kitchen doorway, its deadly fanged chelicerae extended. It charged in, and I threw my knife at its eyes.

It howled in pain, rolling on the living room floor. Grabbing Ben's hand, I dashed back out into the hall and through to the kitchen. Weapons. I grabbed another knife and handed a second one to Ben. I took up watch by the door. "Just try it!" I yelled as the spider pulled itself off the carpet. "We're ready for you!"

I wished I could take back my words as the spider molted a third time, shedding its exoskeleton and tripling in size again. Now it towered over me, filling the room. It couldn't fit through the doors anymore.

I turned despairingly to Ben. His colour was a little off, but he wasn't screaming. "Did I just see what I thought I saw?"

I nodded. "The widow. She used to be three inches long. She's why I screamed during Science."

"No freaking wonder." Ben still looked shaken. "I came here to help. It rained for a while, then all of the sudden it quit. I wanted to wake you, but Lissa wouldn't let me. Then the weirdest thing happened. She reached out with one hand—and her hand disappeared, first to the wrist, then her arm up to the elbow. Then she took a step forward and the rest of her vanished too as if she'd passed through some invisible curtain. Then her hand came out of the invisible wall thing. I grabbed it, to pull her out, you know. But instead she pulled me in after her and into your dream—I still don't know how. She said I'd have to help you because she had to stop a tree from falling."

"A tree?" The blood left my face in a rush. I had forgotten about that dream. The dream in which the spruce tree began to fall on Dad's head.

"Yeah. Lissa said not to worry because she'd take care of it." Ben changed topic, his face strained. "The fire's getting awfully close, Brianne. It's reached the hill above town. You've got to make it rain soon."

"Feel free." I gestured toward the door. "Kill the spider, and it'll rain. Only for heaven's sake, don't miss. When it molts, it'll triple in size again."

Ben peered out the door. "What if it can't get up? Can it still triple in size?"

I was suddenly very glad of Ben's presence. There'd be no breaking down or surrendering while he was around. "I don't think so." I got excited. "If we cripple its legs...maybe...we'll have to be careful, though." I pointed out the spider's fanged chelicerae where they hung down in front of its mouth like a moving mustache.

"Uh-oh," Ben said. "I don't think the widow intends to just sit back and wait for us to attack. Look."

The spider had turned itself clumsily around and was spinning a big sticky net across the kitchen doorway. The strands were as thick and strong as cables.

"Yuck!" I exclaimed and hastily backed out into the hall. "It's trying to trap us. Quick, before it seals off the other doorway, too, and we have no way of getting to it," I whispered.

I went first on hands and knees. I crouched in the dubious protection of the side of the couch, then slowly peeped over the arm. The widow was concentrating on its web, and I was heartened to see that my frantic blow with the knife had knocked two of its eyes in the bottom row out of commission so its blind side faced us. I motioned to Ben, and we slipped along the wall and hid ourselves in the drapes.

The spider side-stepped and began to web out the entrance to the hall. My knees felt weak. Now we really were trapped. Only now we were trapped in with it, instead of out.

"We can do this." Ben squeezed my hand.

I nodded firmly.

"Surprise attack?" Ben put his mouth close to my ear. "On its blind side?"

I nodded again. "Good luck." I pressed a swift kiss to his lips. We were going to need all of the luck we could get.

"On the count of three. One...two...."

The spider's massive fused head and thorax swung our way. We both tensed, but it passed by, and the spider spoke toward the kitchen. "You might as well give up, Brianne. You'll never kill me now. The fire is at Grantmere, smell the smoke." The spider kept talking, gloating, and this time Ben held up fingers. One...two...three!

We burst out of our hiding place, and instantly the spider abandoned its web and came at us. Time seemed to slow, even as my legs continued to propel me forward. *She'd tricked us.* She'd known where we were the whole time. Spiders, I remembered, had poor eyesight to begin with, and so relied on vibrations to tell them where their prey was.

With two targets to choose from, the widow decided to eliminate the bigger one first. Or maybe there was a part of Sir Jeremy still inside it. In any case, it attacked Ben.

I saw a loop of web fly over Ben's head, saw him raise his arm and slash at it, and then my impetus carried me to safety within the thicket of the spider's legs. I hastily attacked the nearest seven-jointed leg.

At the first cut, it flinched, but it didn't stop. I watched, horrified, as more loops piled over Ben, entangling him in their stickiness as fast as he could hack them off, until his knife hand was too stuck to move. "Got you!" cackled the spider. "This time, you'll stay dead!" Ben thrashed wildly, trying to roll out of range of its the poisonous chelicerae.

If the bite of a tiny black widow one centimeter long had made Ben sick enough to go to the hospital, there was no question that a spider this size could kill.

I sawed harder, and a leg fell twitching to the floor. The spider howled in fury, distracted, but didn't lose its balance.

Quick as a flash, its middle shorter pair of legs grabbed me, lifting me up off the floor in a hairy embrace. It spit intestinal juices at me. A few burning drops splattered on my skin, and I screamed, but most fell harmlessly on the floor or my jeans. Not wanting to be introduced to its sucking stomach, I stabbed upward. It dropped me with another shriek of rage.

It turned, trying to move off me so it could web me, too, and I lunged forward. I came up behind its legs by the narrow connecting pedicel that joined the cephalothorax to the abdomen. If I could sever the two....

The exoskeleton was harder than I expected, and the spider's hairy book lungs breathed in and out uncomfortably close to me. Still, I sawed and hacked at it with all the strength I had.

The spider bellowed and tried to turn on me, but I stayed safely out of reach of its pedipalpi and chelicerae. It skittered around on seven legs, seeming not even to notice the loss of one.

I stuck close, hacking with my knife until, finally, I severed a vessel and transparent blood began to squirt everywhere with each beat of its heart. My hands became slick with blood, but I didn't stop, cutting grimly until I was all the way through.

The abdomen containing its heart and lungs fell to the floor, but the legs still moved, propelling the cephalothorax forward. Despair clenched my heart—what was I going to do now?—and then its brain seemed to get the message, and it keeled over, dead.

I stumbled over its awful hairy leg going to Ben. He was wrapped up tighter than a Christmas present, but alive. Between the two of us we managed to free him from most of the silk threads.

His hair was matted with the stuff, and I was covered with blood and spider parts, but he looked wonderful to me, and I hugged him.

From outside came a rumble of thunder and the sound of pelting raindrops on the window.

We ran outside and played in the rain like children, washing ourselves free of gore. The force of the downpour blanked out the red glow from the fire. Soon it would go out altogether. There would be no disaster.

"You did it!" Ben yelled. He framed my face in his hands and kissed me. I drank in cool rain and kissed him back, my body pressed against his.

Lissa woke us up with loud and enthusiastic cheers. My own cheers died when I opened my eyes to bright lights and no rain. I was just about to either start bawling or try to go back into the dream when Lissa shoved a jar with an eight-legged arachnid in my face.

She was jumping up and down with excitement. "Kill the spider! Kill the spider!"

There was a small silence while Ben and I looked at each other. How had she known about the spider? I shrugged. How had she always known?

I put the spider down on the floor and killed it. I ground it into the floor with my foot making very sure it was dead and, above all, giving it no chance to triple in size. Just in case.

The rain came.

Ben swung Lissa up in the air, laughing.

It took time, of course, for even the fiercest downpour to have an effect on such a large fire. The popup fire near the highway succumbed first, but most people simply turned around and drove back to Grantmere.

We listened to radio reports all afternoon. The rain had come a little too late for some. The foothill on the east side of town was the worst hit, suffering a deep burn that had seared the humus in the forest floor leaving only white ash. Six houses on the hill had also burned, but by "some strange freak of wind" Huxton's remained untouched, green lawns and fountains intact in a charred sea. The announcer remarked on the irony that Huxton's owner had died of a stroke that morning.

A fireguard around Grantmere held off the main brunt of the fire with no nearby trees to fall across and breach it. But flying sparks had started a block of buildings on fire. With no reservoir, the firefighters were largely powerless till the rain came.

The heat caused the pavement to buckle and burn as tarred over cracks caught fire. I remembered my vision of burning pavement and shivered.

The first news of deaths came then, a volunteer firefighter who hadn't been equipped with a mask and had succumbed to asphyxiation. Others were reported to be in hospital with varying degrees of burns. The announcer spoke warmly of the bravery of those who had gone back into the hell of heat and smoke to search for overcome comrades. Among those whom he cited was Rex Tremont.

Ben couldn't believe it, and I spent about half an hour filling him in on how Rex had changed sides this morning. I also had to tell him about Sir Jeremy being behind his twin's murder.

"And you're sure he's dead?" Ben asked.

"Yes," I said. "He died of a stroke in the real world this morning, and again in the dream world when we killed the spider. Chris and Aunt Elise have justice."

That evening, when the fire was well and truly dead and the rain still fell, an exhausted but exuberant Mom, Dad and Suzy showed up.

Dad was limping slightly. When I asked him about it, he said a snag had fallen on him. "It nearly fell right on top of me. It would have, but I thought I saw Lissa. I turned toward her just as it crashed." He laughed, and I forced a smile. "Must have been the shock, huh?" He ruffled Lissa's hair. "Thanks all the same."

Mom started talking about another close call that Rex had prevented. She sounded very impressed by Rex's "cool, calm thinking" in an emergency situation. Now that the danger was past she talked as if the fire had been nothing more than a small blaze.

Suzy excused herself brusquely. "I'm exhausted. I'm going to bed." I silently thought she probably didn't want to hear any more about Rex.

Her plan worked. Not only did she miss Mom's compliments, but half an hour later she missed Rex himself when he showed up wanting to see her. His clothes were dishevelled, and his hair looked more brown than blond.

"I'm sorry," I said truthfully. "But she's asleep right now. Can I take a message?"

Rex looked at me blankly, raking his fingers through his hair. He came to a decision. "Yes, you can. Tell her goodbye. If I stay here, the wulfdraigles will use her as a hostage against my behaviour. I'm going to try to lose the wulfdraigles among the thousands of dreamers in a city. I'm through being a conduit."

Sadly, I watched him leave. I felt sorry for him and for Suzy.

Ben put his arm around my shoulders and hugged me. I smiled at him, and he smiled back. A burst of happiness filled my heart. It was over.

Grantmere was saved, and I had a feeling I wasn't ever going to dream again. The black widow had said she was my last dream. More importantly I had *dreamed* it was my last dream, and my dreams always came true.